The Highway Man

Susan C. Barto

THIRD EDITION

©opyright 2003, 2008, 2013 by Susan C. Barto

Library of Congress Control Number:
2003105264

ISBN-10: 0-9712516-9-X
ISBN-13: 9780971251694

Gary Drury's Publishing™

Kentucky

Produced in The United States of America.

DEDICATION

To Harry and Bill.

CONTENTS

LIZ AND JIM

Liz grew up knowing about her difference from other girls. For one thing she lived in a tiny house in a ritzy neighborhood filled with imposing Tudor and Colonial homes, and she guessed that ill will surrounded her parents' building their small, white ranch house on a corner lot in this area. She realized that her interest in classical music and her musical ability that took the form of a trained soprano voice and talent on the piano set her apart from the other teen girls. Only her interest in dramatics could be shared with her friends. When she peered In the mirror she saw that her looks, too, differed from the norm. She possessed long, silky white-blonde hair and a sexy figure that curved in and out without being too ample. She thought her face ordinary but pleasant and seemed surprised when her friends told her they thought her beautiful.

She met her first friend shortly after moving into the new white ranch house. A friendly, attractive dark-haired girl named Sue rang her doorbell and introduced herself one afternoon, Apparently she met with Sue's approval as

Sue introduced her to her group of friends, and they accepted her with smiles. Fortunately, she liked Sue too and immediately discovered that Sue loved dramatics as much as she did and not only belonged to the Drama Club but as its secretary took the minutes at the meetings. Sue gave her instructions as to how to get admitted inside the walls of this exclusive fortress of a club, and soon Liz passed the tryouts and became a fellow member. Liz's given name, Anna Marie, the other girls deemed pretty, they said, but too formal. One day over at Sue's house Sue quipped, "Since you are our town's answer to Elizabeth Taylor let's call you Liz."

Liz loved the nickname instantly, and to her surprise the name stuck. Soon the whole school including the teachers called her Liz. Her parents, however, objected to the appellation, but apparently gave in when they realized that they stood alone on the issue. They continued to call her Anna Marie, but ceased fussing at her friends when they called on the phone or asked at the door for Liz. Liz felt grateful that so many things came easily to her. Her musical talent she claimed as a gift from God, and she worked hard for her dramatic ability. She fared well with her schoolwork, and she enjoyed her success and friends gratefully. Her parents had been opera stars and kept their musical interests up by attending operas and concerts. She sometimes invited Sue to attend concerts with her and her family, and Sue seemed to appreciate the diversion. Liz felt that she with her long blonde hair and Sue with her short, curly black hair made a nice contrast, and many of the boys at school commented on It. One afternoon while walking home from school Sue said, "Liz you always play the field. I've never seen you head over heels with anyone. You seem to care equally for all the boys you date."

"Yes, Sue, that's true. I guess I haven't been bitten hard enough to moon over anyone yet the way you pine over Harry."

Shortly after Liz uttered those words that came to be called famous last words by Sue, Liz herself fell and fell hard for a boy named Jim. Liz had obtained the starring role in the school's yearly musical, "Where's Charley"" and during rehearsals she met a junior year boy named Jim who co-starred with her. Although Liz, a senior, never dated junior year boys she thought Jim an exception. For Liz he epitomized her idea of a Beatnik with his stated love of literature and drama and his idolization of Maron Brando as an actor along with Maron's training in method acting at the famous New York school. Liz respected Jim's words thinking everything he expounded on profound. In addition to acting in the musical with him and the

closeness of rehearsals she sat next to him in her Creative Writing class. Sue sat just behind the two of them. One day Sue told Liz, "Jim gave me super advice regarding the story I'm writing. I think he's talented in all the arts. I don't have to ask you what you think of him, do I?"

"I know, Sue. He told me how he helped revamp your story. Isn't he the school's closest approximation to a Bohemian? He's even read ON THE ROAD. He loaned it to me, and I'll give it to you when I finish. I think he's cool."

Sue laughed at Liz's words, and Liz knew that Sue and the rest of her friends seemed to be aware of her feelings for him Liz hoped that they approved. Not that it would have mattered to Liz. However, Liz felt that Jim needed all the allies he could get in the high school. She knew he could be thought to be as different as she saw herself. For Jim had a severe rash that came and went. His handsome looks suffered from this rash for which he seemed to have no cure. Liz minded the school's gossip about his skin condition empathizing most with him when the kids mocked his parents' failure to get him to a specialist as if they didn't care about his welfare.

"Where's Charley?" turned out to be a smash, and the musical's popularity apparently cemented Liz's popularity as she found herself sought after, and Jim's popularity seemed to soar as he earned the appellation of being her boyfriend. Maybe due to his new success of his relationship with her, Liz delighted in noticing that his rash vanished for this period. At any rate the disappearance of the rash stopped the torrents of gossip surrounding him, and Liz rejoiced in their relationship. For the first time she understood the dither her friends entered when they languished with love for the boys in their lives. She felt elevated by her intimacy with Jim. When she found herself alone with Jim she entered a world that enveloped her with its uniqueness. She and Jim discussed art and literature and the meaning of life. He boosted her spirits and lifted them to a new realm. She thought that with Jim she ceased to worry about the trivial things about which her friends seemed to fret. She knew that Jim could hold his own with anyone, and this proved true as Sue said one afternoon as they walked home from school, "Harry and I would like to double with you and Jim some Saturday night."

As Harry attended college, Liz saw this as a compliment to Jim's intelligence and said so Sue replied, "Jim teaches me things about my duel passions, literature and drama. I'm sure that Harry would find him interesting too."

As Liz's senior year escalated she knew her relationship with Jim might crumble. She had applied to Oberlin because of her musical talent, and Jim had another year of high school facing him before he could enter the world whose threshold she now stood upon. Jim showed enough confidence in himself to keep from looking jealous or worried about losing her. However, Liz knew that the two of them would have to reach a decision about the exclusiveness of their relationship and whether or not each could date others when their forced separation arrived. On the day she received her acceptance to Oberlin Liz drove her car over to Jim's house. She wanted to tell him before letting her parents or Sue know. He looked worried when he saw her on his doorstep.

"Liz, Hi, what's up?'

"Jim, it happened. I got an acceptance to Oberlin."

"Cool. You deserved it. I never worried that you wouldn't get in."

They got In Liz's car and went for a ride to their town's nearby Watchung Reservation with its privacy and cool foliage. The conversation Liz had dreaded appeared to be inevitable, Jim made it easy for Liz. Before she could broach the subject he said, "Liz, you can't enter college tied down to the boy back home. Oberlin is too far from New Jersey for us to have a long distance steady relationship. I cheerfully release you from any bonds and encourage you to join in the campus life including dating."

"Jim, you're too good - a saint."

"Far from it. I just want to play fair. I know I'll miss you terribly and won't be entirely free from the pangs of the green-eyed monster."

As spring turned into summer worries about leaving Jim behind troubled Liz enough to mar her summer. Even the fourth of July with its circus, parties, and fireworks didn't match up to the expectations she'd held for it before she received her acceptance. Sue and her other girlfriends tried to cheer her up, showing that they understood about facing a separation from the one you cared about. Sue threw a party after the fireworks that they'd both attended with their dates and only invited the four of them so that Liz and Jim could have some special time. Many of Liz's girlfriends also faced different colleges' parting them from their boyfriends. Liz realized that her dilemma seemed common enough to many of the senior girls. She knew that her problem resided on a higher level than her friends' problems as she and Jim had a cerebral partnership in addition to the sexual one she knew her friends had. Jim cheered her up at every turn and soon managed to get her anticipating the fall and her new life style. He appeared so skillful at putting a bright face on everything that she wondered how much she'd wounded him if he told the truth. The summer's end brought an halt to the casual routine of Liz's high school days, and the good-bye party Sue threw at the end of August looked to Liz as the last normal event in her life. She savored all of it. She had a feeling of foreboding regarding her relationship with Jim, and she didn't know why. She didn't believe he'd surrender to someone else's allure. Was it herself she doubted?"

Jim drove her to the airport, and her parents kissed her goodbye back at the house. She felt a final wrench when she kissed him good-bye, but she tried to look serene and hopeful. She never would have guessed the excitement that filled her when she glimpsed the campus, settled into her room, and met her roommates. Being with people who cared about music as passionately as she did came as a revelation. Even Jim with all his brilliance possessed little musical ability. In the musical he talked his songs as he'd been chosen for his dramatic ability. Liz found herself spending hours playing the piano and even doing some composing while her voice lessons escalated as she began to understand music theory. She became friendly with other musical people and got involved with a boy who wanted to be an opera star as she did. Days and weeks spun by without her giving a thought to Jim. When the realization of this hit her, she felt sad. How could she abandon someone who had shared her soul's thoughts with her? Her first crush, and how easily she'd tossed him aside. She felt no longing to be with him. She no longer counted the days until Thanksgiving break. She hoped that he'd found another, but somehow she didn't think so. Would she be poised enough to handle their reunion?

Jim in met her at the airport the day before Thanksgiving. Liz had mixed feelings. She seemed able to continue their easy rapport immediately, but her romantic glow had vanished. Jim talked freely about his senior year and acted as though he genuinely wanted to hear all about her college life both on the campus and off it.

"Liz, how does it feel being together now after all this time?"

"Jim, it feels special to be here with you, my first love."

"Oh, first love. That sounds ominous. Does that mean your first love has been replaced with a second?"

"No, it just means that I want you to know that you and our friendship have a special place in my heart for now and always. I hope you feel this way too. Have you been dating as we decided?"

When Jim didn't answer right away, Liz knew that he'd grasped the import of what she had attempted to relay. She would always hold him dear to her heart, but for now she wanted to be free to reach the skies with her musical ambitions and maybe even romantic ones too. She hoped that their connection would fade and then dim rather than blacking out all at once. The glow of his presence still warmed her, and she wanted to withdraw from him slowly. Maybe. they could be friends for some time to come. Hopefully, always. She knew too much to express any desire for friendship. Rather, she stayed silent and still allowing him the freedom to rage if he needed to. His anger would have been easier to bear than his stony silence. He remained stoic as always.

Liz's wishes came true as Jim spent as much of his free time this vacation and on the following ones with her as possible. He didn't push her, and gradually the connection between them changed to a platonic one. Liz knew that even when he left for college across the country they would remain close. Liz would always hold warm thoughts of Jim and how he'd opened up her life and shared her secret thoughts and dreams. She remained grateful to him for helping her grow and flourish even though it meant blossoming without him. She learned that the feelings of nostalgia and affection for her first love would never leave her. She hoped that Jim could take away strength from their romance too. She also knew that Jim's maturity enabled him to hide whatever pain she might have caused him and never make her feel uncomfortable about his loss. A relationship as perfect as theirs had been could leave only good memories behind.

JANETTE

When Susie first met Jan she thought Jan looked exactly like the girl on the Sunshine Bread package - blond pigtails and an adorable face. Jan later told her that she instantly thought upon meeting Susie that Susie looked beautiful with all that curly black hair. Susie remembered their first meeting as like at first sight. Immediately, they were bonded and remained cemented together as best friends until something mysterious happened.

In grade school both girls belonged to the same set of friends, and they became even closer in junior high school. Although here in junior high school they each made a bunch of friends and even started a group of their own, the two of them retained the best friend designation. The girls in their group possessed friendly attitudes - this was a group not a clique. All over the school that seventh grade year (the first in junior high) groups were in the process of forming. Best of all Susie and Jan lived only a block from each other and could, therefore, walk home together and even more importantly run to school in the mornings because they both tended to be in danger of being tardy each day.

Early on in their friendship Susie and Jan shared secrets. One of Jan's secrets turned out to be that her first name was really Janette. Susie felt Janette to be exotic and enigmatic name and although she kept Jan's secret, she thought of Jan as Janette in her mind and sometimes it' none of the other girls could overhear she called her by that name. Susie and Jan doubled dated went to slumber parties, and spent overnights at each other's houses. Their mothers must have felt as though they had two daughters. Fortunately, each girl had two beds in her bedroom so giggling overnights proved to be no problem. One of the most fun things they did together was baby-sitting. While each had her own regulars, frequently they both baby-sat

together if this turned out to be convenient for their regulars. Susie seemed to get baby-sitting jobs more frequently than Jan and often they double baby-sat at Susie's favorite adopted family the Parkers who had two darling boys, Teddy and David. One night while perusing Mrs. Parker's college yearbook, Susie discovered that Mrs. Parker must be 32 years old.

"Poor thing," Jan exclaimed when Susie showed her.

The double baby-sitting gigs paid off big time when the Parkers asked Susie if she'd like to come along to Bayhead at the New Jersey shore for two weeks of the coming summer and bring Jan. Susie, thrilled right down to the solcs of her feet, couldn't wait to let Jan know. Jan didn't disappoint.

"Bayhead. Wait till the other girls hear about this they'll be green with envy."

"Maybe the girls," Susie answered. "Don will be furious. We just began going steady two weeks ago."

"Well, Susie, It's only for two weeks. You'll both survive."

Their friends expressed their envy to Susie's satisfaction, and Don had to be away the same two weeks anyway so nothing remained except planning the big event. The surf and sun turned out to be perfect, their duties light, and Susie felt that she couldn't ask for more. She didn't even feel jealous when a handsome lifeguard asked Jan out on the second Thursday off as she still wore Don's ring and honored her commitment. The first Thursday off she and Jan had shared and had gone to the boardwalk and spent one of the happiest days Susie had ever experienced. She looked forward to going home and seeing Don and even starting school.

Once home Susie's world began to crash in pieces around her. First she discovered that Don had cheated on her over the summer after she'd tried so hard to only flirt but not date. Worse than that, however, she faced a mystery in her life. Jan had departed for a family vacation just before school started, and Susie missed her especially now because of Don's betrayal. On the day that Jan returned Susie called her as soon as she saw the family car ride up their driveway.

"Hi, Jan. I'm so glad you're back. I missed you terribly. You'll never believe what that creep Don did"'

"Susie, I can't talk now. I'll call you back."

But she didn't call back. Not that day nor for the rest of the years Susie remained in high school. When the girls met face to face Jan either turned her face away from Susie's or behaved as though Susie were invisible. Susie's hurt surpassed any hurt she'd ever received before. Break ups with boyfriends while unpleasant at least could be expected. But shouldn't a best friend be for life? Worst of all for Susie, Jan's behavior divided their group of friends in half with the girls who felt closer to Jan staying with her (although so far as Susie knew Jan never explained to anyone) and the girls who felt closer to Susie staying with her. One of the latter tried over and over to telephone Jan to find out what this could be all about, but reported to Susie that she'd had no success.

Although the incident occurred when Susie and Jan belonged to the ninth grade class, it had ramifications lasting all the way to graduation from high school and even beyond. When Susie was a sophomore in high school she dated a senior boy who lived next door to Jan. Apparently, Susie discovered, Jan had a crush on this boy. Since by now the two groups had no contact with one another Susie had been ignorant about this. The entire time that Susie dated Steve Jan spread rumors that he'd really asked her out first, and she'd declined. Eventually everything came to a head when Jan's mother told Steve that since he'd only moved to their town a few months ago he wouldn't be able to go to the spring country club dance unless she or another member of the committee approved him. She continued by saying that if he took Jan to the dance she'd approve him and if not, he couldn't go to the dance at all.

What a mess this made for Susie. She told Steve to go to the dance with Jan and that she'd go with someone else. "Maybe we'll be able to dance together once we get there," she said to Steve and started considering other invitations. She accepted an invitation from Bob who danced better than anyone else in the school. By now she felt more angry than hurt with Jan. To Susie's surprise, the dance ended up being quite special. She danced with her own date and also with Steve who danced more dances with her than he did with Jan. To add to the fun, Susie walked on the country club grounds in the soft spring night first with Bob and then with Steve. She asked whether he enjoyed being with Jan.

"Sure, she's all right. But, she's either wearing a strange perfume or she smells like sweat."

Susie felt just mad enough at Jan to enjoy this rather crude remark. and she said nothing and tried hard not to smile.

Soon after the dance Steve's graduation day arrived. Susie felt disappointed because she had no ticket to go since each family only received four tickets, and Steve's family needed all four. In the early afternoon of the graduation the doorbell rang and when Susie answered it she saw Jan's older sister, Joann, standing on her doorstep holding a ticket to the graduation.

"Susie, as you know I'm graduating tonight along with Steve, and I have an extra ticket. Please take it"

Susie felt too shocked to protest, and she knew instinctively not to ask Joann why she came here with the ticket. "Thank you, Joann, I'll never forget this," she said and then allowed herself to feel joy.

Sometime during Susie's senior year in high school Jan started going steady with a hunk named Terry. Whether this formed the catalyst for a small change in Jan's attitude or whether it was unconnected Susie didn't know. Jan was appointed the chairman of the yearbook committee and the one in charge of the savings under the pictures. Susie feared that because of this, Jan night attack once more by putting belittling remarks under Susie's picture. She knew the remarks couldn't be overt, but still she worried. However, when the yearbook came out the words under her name turned out to be ones she'd have chosen herself. After all, no one knew her as well as she believed Jan did.

About two years after graduation when Susie was engaged and had graduated from Katherine Gibbs and taken some college courses she bumped into Jan downtown.

"Hi, Susie. I read in the paper that you're engaged. Congratulations. Are you going to be home tonight?"

"Yes, why?"

"Come for dinner. Mother would be thrilled to see you."

Thinking that this would finally solve the mystery that had managed to cloud her high school life, Susie accepted eagerly.   Jan's family did seem pleased to see her, and from the way, everyone behaved Susie felt that they were trying to act like nothing had ever happened.

After dinner Jan and Susie went to Jan's room for a gab session. Now, Susie thought I'll ask her.

"Jan, why did you suddenly just stop talking to me at the end of our last summer in junior high?"

But she received no satisfaction. Jan merely looked at her as though she were puzzled and said,

"I don't know what you mean."

Susie realized that impossible as it seemed, Jan had either forgotten or blocked the whole incident from her mind. For a moment the only thing Susie could come up with burst forth without her knowing why,

"Oh, Janette, you're still as much of an enigma as your name."

That was the last time she ever saw Jan although Jan called her at the time of the class's tenth reunion. She said she'd just become divorced and asked Susie whether she ought to go. Although Susie encouraged her to go Jan never showed. Another unsolved mystery only this time Susie didn't try to solve it.

THE HIGHWAY MAN

Susannah wanted to be chosen for the Drama Club. From the first time she'd ever heard of this magic club, she'd longed to be inside of its exclusive doors. Most of her friends had dreamed of being cheerleaders since grade school and especially after they started attending football games in junior high, and Susannah's best friend, Jean, wanted to be a twirler. She wanted to be a twirler so badly that she bought a baton and carried it with her everywhere she went from the first day of junior high. She practiced twirling constantly even letting Susannah's dog, Trinket. escape through the back door when one of the new neighborhood dogs was in heat because she twirled her baton as Trinket lunged through the open door where she was practicing. Susannah's father, furious with Jean as he didn't want Trinket's being accused of fathering that female dog's puppies, almost forbade her the house. The incident never stopped Jean's whirling so much as a missed beat.

Susannah's passion for acting exceeded even Jean's love for twirling. She'd participated in every grade school play in her memory, and her dreams and goals all centered upon being an actress. This sophisticated and mysterious Drama Club only allowed members who'd passed the try-outs. First of all, one had to be a sophomore to even be allowed to try out. Susannah knew that an applicant for membership had to do a dramatic

reading of his or her choice and then be assigned a panto-mime to do on a second's notice. The creative writing and dramatics teacher, Mr. Deeds, and a chosen few of the most talented members of the club would be judging the event. Most dramatic of all the steps leading to acceptance in this coveted circle Susannah knew centered on the Drama Club's method of letting new members know they had joined this club. On the Monday morning following the try-outs, each selected new member would find a small white envelope containing an invitation on his or her desk during homeroom. The rest of the applicants would have to wait another year before being able to try out again for the club.

Susannah saw the awaited-for notice for try-outs to the Drama Club tacked to the community bulletin board in the hall the first week of her sophomore year. The try-outs had been scheduled for one week from the time of the notice's posting. Susannah skipped home from school, charged into the house and yelled,

"Mother!"

"Hi, dear. What is it?"

The drama club try-outs are being held a week from today. Should I read something from Inge's "Picnic?" Or maybe Tennessee Williams?"

25

"I don't think so, dear. What about reading a poem?"

"Oh, Mother. You and poetry. I think poetry is dumb, and it's not half as dramatic as one of the readings I mentioned."

"Did you ever read "The Highwayman" by Alfred Noyes?"

"No, I never even heard of it."

"Here let me get my poetry anthology. Hear the poem through to the end before you reject it."

While Susannah put a bored expression on her face she watched her mother's expression become rapt as she began to read.

> The wind was a torrent of darkness
> Among the gusty trees,
> The moon was a ghostly galleon
> Tossed upon cloudy seas.
> The road was a ribbon of moonlight
> Over the purple moor,
> And the highwayman came riding—
> Riding— riding—
> The highwayman came riding,
> Up to the old inn-door.

On the words poured from her mother's throat, and Susannah found herself caught up in the throes of the drama's being recited. The romantic highwayman falls in love with a bonny landlord's daughter, and he asks her to watch for him by moonlight.

I'll come to thee by moonlight though hell I should bar the way.

Meanwhile King George's men, who are chasing the highwayman, tie the lovely Bess up and bind a musket beneath her breast telling her to watch for the highwayman. When at last she heard his horse's hoofs ringing, she felt desperate to warn her lover. She shot herself with the musket beneath her breast and with her death warned him. Still they say you can hear the highwayman riding by moonlight towards the landlord's blackeyed daughter who plaits a Red love-knot into her gorgeous black hair. By the time her mother had finished the poem, Susannah had broken into tears. What a dramatic poem. If this didn't get the judges, nothing would. After hearing and absorbing the poem she turned to her mother and hugged her.

Hours of practice followed this decision. How to convey the drama of the poem without turning it into a melodrama calling for hissing and booing. Over and over she read the poem aloud trying for just the right amount of pathos without her voice's turning it into bathos. By the day of the try-outs she felt ragged and grateful that her voice hadn't gone from the constant practicing. When her name was called she centered herself on the stage and read the poem with all the feelings that had washed upon her when she heard her mother read the poem. With such a romantic reading she half expected to be stopped midway through the first few stanzas. However, she read all the way to the climax before Mr. Deeds stopped her. He said nothing about her performance, and wordlessly handed her a slip of paper requesting her to perform a pantomime of a girl who slowly realizes that she's been stood up on a date. Susannah had never been stood up on a date in her young life, but she'd imagined the possibility frequently. The idea seemed so horrible that the thought had occurred to her often. Forgetting that pantomime terrified her, she just acted out without words the feelings that coursed through her as she empathized with the girl's realizing that her boyfriend might actually not show. She pretended to read, looked up furtively at the clock and at her wrist-watch, and finally allowed herself to despair. The dramatics teacher waited until her performance had ended before stopping her with a simple, "Thank you."

The next few days felt like torture. Nothing her friends did or talked about seemed important. No television program or book, and certainly no homework assignment transfixed her enough to move her mind away from the audition and its possible outcomes. The Monday following the try-outs finally dawned, and Susannah dawdled all the way to school her footsteps dragging down the halls toward her homeroom. She wanted to put off the probable rejection for as long as possible. After so many years of looking forward to joining the Drama Club the pivotal moment had finally arrived, and she felt too frightened to let her glance go near her desk. She'd had nightmares for days about seeing the desktop empty. When she finally allowed her eyes to alight on the desk she couldn't believe the sight that greeted her. Shining bright and pristine white in the corner of the desk lay the coveted invitation. She'd made it. For the rest of, her high school career she could belong to the Drama Club without ever trying out again. Thank you God.

In spite of her up to this point dismal feelings about poetry and how it compared to drama and literature, she knew she'd always have an affectionate soft feeling come over her when she heard "The Highwayman". Its drama, corny or no, had propelled her to just where she wanted to land. She'd plopped right into her cloud of deepest wishes, and there she hoped to stay in as long as possible. The Drama Club proved to be her niche in high school just as she'd known it would be, and she counted many of her fellow Drama Club members among her closest friends.

SNOW DAYS

Whenever it began to snow on Sunday nights Carol Lee's father would chuckle and tell his hopeful daughter and her brother, "They won't close the schools. It won't snow hard enough. Better pray for a blizzard. Lots of luck."

Carol Lee and her brother, Don, laughed at their father. Carol Lee knew the snow would continue to fall. Right now the snow looked deep enough to grab their sleds and head out the door where some of the kids were sleigh riding down the hill next door always kept lit by street lights. Carol Lee dashed up the hill carrying her sled and flung herself onto the sled belly first. She exhilarated in the feeling of flying down the hill heedless of cars that might be lurking at the bottom, feeling her brown braids whip out from under her wool cap.

"Go, Carol Lee," she heard Don yell. "I'm coming down right after you."

When Carol Lee came back to the house later on feeling cold and tired her arm linked with Don's who must have felt the same way, their mother gave them steaming hot cups of cocoa with marshmallows on top. She concurred with the children that it might snow furiously enough to close school tomorrow. With a prayer for a blizzard on her lips, Carol Lee fell into sleep dreaming of snowmen. When she woke in the morning the world looked white and the glare coming through the windows seemed enough to blind her. She peered out the window and saw magnificent drifts and piles of snow some as high as the living room window. Lacy ice patches had formed in the trees, and the roofs of the houses had been touched by Jack Frost. Apparently snow had poured down and created a wonderland of white. She couldn't see the sidewalks or even the streets.

"Mom, Mom," she called. Put on WOR on the radio. School must be out today."

"Yeah, Mom, Carol Lee's right," shouted Don. Maybe the announcer on WOR will confirm that Summit's schools are closed today."

"All right. But your father's gone to work already. He must have reached the station since he's not come back."

Mere minutes after their mother put the radio on, Carol Lee and Don heard the announcer mention Summit schools as being closed. Carol Lee whooped out joy, and Don cried out cheers. They wound up in the living room where the picture window overlooked the results from the storm. Coming toward their house down the street Carol Lee spied their next door neighbor Peter.

"Look," she laughed. "It's Peter from next door. He must have gone all the way to school not realizing that they closed it. What a dope!"

31

"Let's see," said Don. "He actually walked all the way to the high school. That's the funniest thing I've ever seen."

The two children roared with laughter, and they laughed until they shook with mirth. The idea that anyone could have actually thought school would be open in the middle of a blizzard tickled Carol Lee's fancies. For the rest of her life just the mention of Peter's snowy walk home from the closed school could set Carol Lee off in gales of laughter. Peter looked like a nerd anyway, and he actually liked school. Who else would be dumb enough or anxious enough to go to school to leave the warmth of his own hearth to attempt to get to the school on a day like this? This day seemed to be made for lounging around all morning watching the quiz shows on television and then heading for the nearby hill for more sledding. Their whole neighborhood's children engaged in sledding and would probably be gathered at the hill next door for most of the afternoon after a lazy morning. Their mother cooked a special breakfast of golden scrambled eggs and crispy bacon and even cinnamon toast to celebrate the occasion. Carol Lee felt festive almost like Christmas. Before heading to the hill with their sleds, Carol Lee and Don stayed in their own front yard long enough to build a snowman. They tried making him look nerdy, and decided to name him Peter.

"Wind him up, and he walks to school," chuckled Don.

Though Carol Lee lived through many snow days like this one, the snow days that lay embedded in her brain came one year in her childhood during a blizzard that some called an ice storm. Many called it the storm of the century or at least of the decade. Not only did the sky dump mountains and great drifts of snow on the world, but the ice caused power to shut down. Without heat or lights for a whole week, the world became an alien, but not altogether terrible environment. Fortunately, Carol Lee's family had a gas stove, a fireplace, and many candles and kerosene lamps in the house. The neighborhood families who owned electric stoves had to eat their meals at other peoples' houses. Carol Lee's family played host to the Smith family from the next block who like many others had an electric stove. Each night at dinner time, Mr. and Mrs. Smith and their three children, two of whom Carol Lee and Don had as friends, came to their house. Carol Lee's mother cooked hardy meals each night for the whole crew. After dinner they all gathered around the fireplace and toasted marshmallows. Carol Lee found much of this week exciting, but she hated reading by candlelight or the kerosene lamp. She wondered how Abraham Lincoln had managed to end up so smart if he'd had to do his reading in that log cabin by candlelight. Reading formed much of Carol Lee's life, and she disliked having the bulk of her reading confined to the daylight hours. Especially since just before the big storm, as this had been a snowy winter, the town officials had installed a wooden hill at Memorial Field just a block or so from Carol Lee's house. This gave the children a steeper and safer place to ride their sleds than her neighboring hill. The hill seemed so steep that each ride down it on her stomach both frightened and revved Carol Lee up. Each time she tramped through the deep layers of snow to the top of the hill she felt apprehension mingled with an almost feverish anticipation. She spent most of the days of that week of the blizzard sledding down the wooden hill arriving home red-cheeked and chilled down to and through her wool socks. Her mother removed her mittens and chafed her red hands and always offered hot chocolate. Her mother seemed preoccupied this week with all the extra cooking and the worrying about Mrs. Smith. Mrs. Smith, in her ninth month of pregnancy, showed signs of having the baby at any moment. Fortunately, Carol Lee's father owned a jeep with four wheel drive should the emergency arrive, but Carol Lee guessed that her mother hoped fervently that the need should not arrive during the week that the Smith's dined with them. However, Carol Lee herself felt excited about the forthcoming birth and prayed that the baby's arrival would take place during this topsy-turvy week of the great white blizzard. The week had neared its end without Mrs. Smith's going into labor, and it looked as though Carol Lee would just have to miss this momentous event. However on Friday evening of that snow filled week as the two families toasted marshmallows before the roaring fire, Mrs. Smith let out a yelp of pain that startled the rest of the group.

"Tom," she said to her husband. "This is it."

Carol Lee's father warmed up the jeep, and he and Mr. Smith escorted Mrs. Smith to the hospital leaving Carol Lee's mother home with the children. Carol Lee's nerves jumped at each sound as she fervently hoped that she wouldn't have to go to bed before the new baby arrived.

"Mother, may I stay up until the baby comes?"

"I don't know, Carol Lee, it might not even happen until morning. However, this is Mrs. Smith's fourth child so maybe it will come quickly. We might know before your bedtime."

Don showed little interest in waiting up for the baby and spent the time snacking and drinking endless cokes.

He said that he minded the loss of the TV tremendously. Carol Lee thought that Mrs. Smith's going into labor at her house might be the most exciting event of her life. Although Don professed to hardly care about babies, Carol Lee had always loved babies and never minded baby-sitting after school. She looked forward to the time when she'd be old enough for her mother to allow her to sit at night as well as in the afternoon. Carol Lee attempted to read by the light of three candles, but she couldn't concentrate because of her nervousness. Just as it turned eleven o'clock, and she knew her mother would send her to bed she heard the crunch of the jeep's tires in the snow, and then her father's tread on the front stairs.

"Hey, is everyone awake?"

"We almost went up to bed," Carol Lee's mother answered.

What happened? Did she have the baby yet?"

"She sure did. An eight pound boy whom they named Mike."

"Oh, Daddy, that's great. Just think I saw her go into labor, and now she has a new baby. Maybe I can baby-sit."

"Hardly," her mother answered. "Remember she has Mary Jane and Betty at home." Although many snow days followed that week of the blizzard in subsequent years, none equaled that snow vacation. All other winters they got just one snow day at a time. One fall while Carol Lee attended high school hurricane warnings came into effect. The radio and TV warned that their area would be hard hit. The school district gave its first hurricane day. As usual Carol Lee experienced her familiar thrill and enjoyed her special day off breakfast in the cozy kitchen anticipating wild weather to follow. After breakfast she and Don wandered into the living room, sat on the picture window cushions and watched for the hurricane and violent winds to begin. Carol Lee hoped that the water might rise high enough to sail a boat down the street as it had one summer. However by 11:00 a.m. the sun shone without even a rainbow since whatever rain there had been had stopped. The sun dazzled, the temperature rose to 75 degrees, and she felt that she'd been given a rare treat. However, the school officials must have felt so stupid about the aborted hurricane that for the remainder of the time Carol Lee spent in high school she never again experienced the myriad pleasures of another snow day. She contented herself with the rich and varied memories of the snow days that had gone before.

ERIC AND THE DUH CLUB

While Eric attended the third grade at Allen Roberts School the children used the latest slang word, Duh, so often that the word came equipped with its own vocabulary approved and selected by the children themselves. When Eric told his mother about the Duh vocabulary she expressed surprise and asked,

"How can a word that isn't even a word have a vocabulary of its own? Who gave it the vocabulary? How did it become official?"

"Oh, Mother. It goes like this, listen: Duh, the main word, then Dar and its offshoot A Dar, then Doy and A Doy and finally De which might even be pronounced just plain Du, half of Duh."

"But, Eric, what does Duh mean in the first place?"

"Oh, Mother. Everyone knows that Duh means stupid or idiotic."

"The only place I ever saw the word was when dumb Moose used it in the "Archie" comics."

"Well that alone dates you. But you see how clear the meaning of the word is?"

One day at the drugstore while his mother purchased a cricket lighter, this incident's happening before she and most other adults gave up smoking for good, Eric took a good look at the picture of the cricket on the lighter's cardboard package. He noted that the cricket was dressed up in top hat and tails and seemed to have doffed along with the outfit a self-satisfied smirk. He looked ridiculous, but also looked as though he thought he looked regal and super-intelligent.

"Mother, look at that cricket. Did you ever see anything or anyone so Duh in your whole life? May I have the cardboard wrapper when you remove the lighter?"

"Of course, but why do you want it?"

"I don't know. But I'll tell you when I figure it out."

Once home he took the wrapper and carefully cut the cricket out. Laughing at the expression on the insect's face, he carefully laid the cardboard bug on his dresser. Later in the evening he mused upon the stupidity of the cricket. The next time he went into the drugstore with his mother he took a careful look at the cricket lighter display. To his delight he discovered that the cricket appeared on different packages wearing different garb but displaying the same Duh smirk as he wore on the original package his mother had purchased.

"Mom, do you or Dad need another lighter? Please."

"Oh, Eric. You mean for the cricket? I think Daddy needs a new lighter. I'll get this for him, but don't remove it from the cardboard wrap until I give it to him. I'm sure he'll be happy to let you have it as soon as he opens the lighter."

The discovery of the different crickets on the lighter packages made Eric anxious to collect them all. He became maddened because his mom and dad wouldn't buy a bunch of lighters all at once so he could complete his collection. Each time he went along to the drugstore he managed to convince his mother to buy just one more. One day the attractive teen-aged girl behind the counter overheard the discussion about the cricket and asked to be filled in. When she heard that Eric had amassed a bunch of these crickets and that his goal would be to have each one she burst into peals of laughter. She'd enjoyed this she said, and also that she didn't know when she'd ever laughed as hard at anything.

One day while going through the trading stamps drawer Eric discovered an old book of King Korn stamps featuring a picture of King Korn himself, possibly the only one in existence at this juncture. Eric felt that if any creature could look as Duh as the cricket it might just be King Korn. What a discovery! He carefully cut the King Korn figure out and gently placed it beside his group of crickets. In the place of honor at the head of this group lay the original cricket in his tux. Now Eric looked for potential members of this now named Duh Club, and shared his discoveries with his mother. The next member Eric chose came from an old record album of his mother's. On the bottom of the record on the back cover were featured two miniature portraits of the pianist. For some reason Eric discovered in the pianist the same combination of superiority and ridiculousness he'd first noticed in the cricket and King Korn. He neatly cut the two cardboard pictures of the pianist and placed them with the other members of his club. An Avon product for children called Duster Duckling who led the Easter parade of Easter values became the next member. At first Eric contented himself with the picture from the Avon booklet, but his mother presented him with the genuine plastic Duster who became the first three-dimensional member of the group. Soon Mr. Peanut from Planters and (tentatively, after the other members had voted) the Wise Potato Chip owl became members. All except for the pianist could be labeled Trademarks. Eric really had a Trademark collection.

Eric's mother formed the annoying habit of using Do as a word in the Duh vocabulary when she should have used Duh or one of the other legal forms of the Duh word. Eric knew that she knew that this annoyed him, and he never let her get away with using the offensive Do without correcting her. Naturally, this seemed to amuse her so much that she kept on using Do to Eric's great upset. One day during a long car ride home from his Aunt's house in Massachusetts Eric's mother used the offensive word once too often, and Eric pronounced that now this meant that she'd been ousted from the official Duh Club. She seemed disappointed and surprised that she'd ever been a member and pleaded with Eric to allow her entrance again if she promised not to use the hated Do. Eric felt tempted and a little sorry for her, but he also felt justified. The best he could do would be to temporarily keep her out until the year 2000, and since this took

place in the bicentennial year of 1976 that seemed eons away. The second thing he planned to do would be to have an election with the Duh Club members voting on the legality of the dreaded Do word. As soon as the family returned home, Eric lined up the paper club members and Duster and held an election. He allowed his mother to watch the results. The cricket and King Korn voted "No", and only one of the copycat crickets and one picture of the pianist voted to allow Do in the club.

"That tears it. Mom. You are out of the club until 2000 unless something drastic comes up."

The next afternoon his mother arrived home from shopping to hear an old-fashioned record playing on the old-fashioned Victor record player Eric owned. The record blasted out a tinny version of "Do Do Doodlie Do". Eric told his mom that this signified that she could rejoin the Duh Club as one of his friends had used Do today at school when he meant Duh, and the word could now officially be part of the vocabulary even if King Korn and the original cricket had voted no. Eric hated seeing his mother unhappy, and his consideration seemed to please her extraordinarily.

One week Eric's Grandmother from Florida came to visit with them. Ordinarily this constituted a treat for Eric as he enjoyed his Grandmother. This visit started out to be as much fun as usual until one Wednesday afternoon when Eric discovered that his Duh Club no longer sat on his dresser in his room.

"Mother," he howled. " Where is my Duh Club? My dresser top's been emptied."

He felt close to tears and mystified as to what on earth could have happened to his beloved Club members. Grandmother heard the rumpus and came running into Eric's room along with Eric's mother.

"Eric, his mother said, "What's the matter?"

Eric said, "Someone's removed my Duh Club. Did you or Grandma throw them away?"

"I didn't throw away any club, just some little pieces of paper and cardboard," Grandmother said.

"Oh, No! When did you throw the pieces of paper away?"

"Yesterday morning. Why?"

"Oh, I hope you threw the papers out after the garbage men came," Eric's mother said and ran outside to rummage through the trash pails.

Unfortunately, the garbage men had been there, and Eric's Duh Club had been dissolved. He could replace the crickets, Mr. Peanut, the Wise Owl, and possibly the pictures of the pianist, but King Korn was lost forever. He tried writing to King's Supermarket Headquarters in search of another one, but he found himself unsuccessful. Duster Duckling still remained (the plastic version), but the small Avon booklet paper member had gone the way of the rest. After this tragedy, Eric lost his taste for collecting Duh Club members. It just didn't seem the same. But he knew his mother retained the same pleasant memories of the crickets, et al., and of the time he had gone out of his way to reinstate her in the Duh Club.

"AUNT" ETHEL

Whenever she wrote to Meg whether sending a birthday card or simply greetings she signed the missals "Aunt" Ethel. Meg understood that "Aunt" Ethel although not related to her by blood enjoyed this honorary title because of love. Meg loved "Aunt" Ethel as she knew her brother Bill did also, and in return "Aunt" Ethel loved them and championed their causes. Her friendship with Meg's parents dated back to when they had been dating and first married. She and her husband Carl along with Meg's parents made up the nucleus of a group of close friends who remained friendly through the years. Actually, the friendship with "Aunt" Ethel continued even after she and her husband Carl got divorced. This put "Aunt" Ethel in the position of being the only divorced person Meg had ever met. Because of the divorce Meg thought that a kind of reverse glamour surrounded "Aunt" Ethel as though she came from a foreign country and spoke a different language. As the custom of the times dictated, their friendship with "Aunt" Ethel following the divorce made it impossible for Meg's parents to continue having a relationship with Carl. During Meg's childhood no fault

divorce and divorce without anger and rancor hadn't yet arrived.

A visit from "Aunt" Ethel carried with it all the anticipation of a holiday. She always unpacked her suitcase shortly after arriving and unearthed presents for Meg and Bill. One dire time although Meg adored her present, a junior manicure kit, "Aunt" Ethel gifted Bill with a realistic rubber snake. Meg had a pathological fear of snakes, even lifelike toy ones, and she knew Bill to be a relentless tease.

Sure enough that very evening after she climbed into bed and snuggled down between the sheets her foot touched something alien. She jumped out of bed and threw down the covers discovering the rubber snake lying on the bottom of the bed. Bill had not showed much patience before acting. She cursed her lack of suspicion. From that day forth and for many years thereafter, Meg never leapt into bed without turning down the counterpane far enough to check for the presence of rubber snakes. Her shrieks upon discovering the intruder in her bed brought her parents and "Aunt" Ethel, and to her relief her father tossed the rubber snake out in the trash. Small punishment. She understood that Bill had enjoyed his trick—listening to Meg's screams must have been well worth the loss of his toy.

"Aunt" Ethel listened endlessly to Meg's triumphs and troubles. Meg's father had a volatile temper, erupting frequently without provocation. One night after a scene between Meg and her father as she, her mother and "Aunt" Ethel washed the dishes; Aunt Ethel gave some advice.

"My mother put up with a lot of guff from my father, and she solved it by smiling agreeably to his face and then sticking her tongue out after he'd left the room. It seemed to help."

Meg smiled hearing this anecdote, and filed it away in a compartment of her mind where she could draw on it if necessary. "Aunt" Ethel seemed like AN OLD FASHIONED GIRL straight out of the Louisa May Alcott novel. Like Alcott's characters, "Aunt" Ethel had proper manners and always wore her skirts long even when fashion dictated otherwise. Meg had read LITTLE WOMEN at least five times, and felt proud to bear the name of its prettiest heroine.

The three other sisters' names ranked high on Meg's list of favorite names. She even used the March sisters' names for the heroines in the short stories she enjoyed writing. One day while visiting her favorite toy store in town, Meg discovered to her joy that Madam Alexander had just created five LITTLE WOMEN dolls, Meg, Jo, Beth, Amy, and their beloved Marmie. She longed to collect those dolls. Never had she wanted something more. She ran home and begged her mother, but as the dolls came with exorbitant price tags, her mother demurred saying,

"Maybe for a special occasion or for one of your favorite aunts to buy you. Show a little patience."

Meg exercised control over her desire to a certain extent, but she couldn't stop showing all her friends the LITTLE WOMEN dolls whenever she could coax them into town and to the toy store. Her friends agreed that yes the dolls looked superior, but that yes they cost too much for them to put them on their own wish lists. Meg seemed stuck with worshipping the dolls from a distance. At least now she had something to hope and strive for. The situation remained stagnant until "Aunt" Ethel's next visit. On the second day of her visit Meg joined her mother and her "aunt" on a jaunt downtown. As they passed the toy store Meg whispered something about the dolls to "Aunt" Ethel.

"LITTLE WOMEN remains one of my favorite books. It influenced my growing up and young womanhood. Let's go in and take a look and see whether Madam Alexander did justice to the characters of the girls and Marmie."

Trembling on the brink of barely concealed joy and hope, Meg led her mother and "Aunt" Ethel into the store and over to her treasures. Even Meg's mother gasped at the beauty and precision of the dolls.

"Aunt" Ethel fell under the same spell that held Meg captive. "Meg, which of the five dolls would you like to have if you could buy one today?"

"That's easy," Meg replied in a shaky voice. "Beth is my favorite character in the book. Each time I reread the book I hope she won't die. But even though I know she always will, she stays my favorite sister."

"Well, what do you say to my buying Beth for you this time around? Maybe I can buy you another someday to celebrate an important milestone like graduating from sixth grade. What do you say?"

Meg had lost her tongue. She wrapped her arms around "Aunt" Ethel in a hug and repeated her thanks over and over like a mantra. Meg's mother didn't lose this opportunity to point out to Meg how lucky she thought her to be to have an "aunt" like this one. However, Meg needed no one's pointing out what a unique part "Aunt" Ethel played in her life. She thought that anyone would be lucky to have her in her life, but that privilege had been granted to her.

She knew that "Aunt" Ethel had no children, and on some level she realized that she and Bill helped fulfill that gap in her life. Meg responded to this by sharing her life's ups and downs with "Aunt" Ethel. Her rewards came with the interest "Aunt" Ethel showed in even the most minute events of Meg's life. She felt special to not only have parents who cared about her welfare, but "Aunt" Ethel who cared without having to. Eventually "Aunt" Ethel obtained all the LITTLE WOMEN dolls for Meg who kept them on a shelf in her room, played carefully with them as she had them act out the novel, and carried the dolls with her after she married carefully preserving them as a precious part of her past. Even after Meg grew to be a woman she continued to correspond with "Aunt" Ethel and considered it a treat when they could get together. "Aunt" Ethel had played the role of fairy godmother to Meg, and Meg wished that everyone could have a guardian angel just like her.

MY BOY BILL

I'd wanted a girl during the nine months of my pregnancy, yet when the doctor yelled, "It's a boy!" I replied "I'm glad." The first time I saw him I felt wonder struck by his white blond hair. Being a brunette myself, I'd always wanted to wake up one day, go to the mirror and discover that my hair had turned blonde overnight. Alas, no such miracle ever happened, but here lay my precious son complete with golden hair. His eyes were my father's knowing eyes in his infant's innocent face. My husband picked him out from among the other babies in the nursery. He said, "As soon as I laid eyes on him I knew he belonged to us."

The first time the nurse presented him to me for feeding, I held him and began bonding instantly. I forget the exact words I crooned to him, but now I felt protective of all new born babies and stories of abandoned and deserted babies upset me beyond reason. The tiger cat's protective instinct forms in the instant a mother cradles her new-born and never leaves her for as long as her child lives. My memories of that short interlude in the hospital carry with them the scent of roses. Harry, my husband, brought a dozen red roses as did my father who tried to outdo Harry by sending long-stemmed roses. My boss sent pink roses, and my brother yellow. Surrounded by the fragrance and beauty of the June flowers, my birth flowers, I luxuriated in the love coming my way from my husband, parents, relatives and friends. And what had I done to deserve all this approval and welcome positive regard? I'd given birth to a beautiful son causing me to feel like a child on Christmas morning who's just received a doll she had coveted but never hoped to receive.

With his blond hair he looked like sunshine when he wore yellow, and he wore it a good deal since we didn't know the sex of an expected baby back in 1963 and tended to buy yellow layettes or mint green ones. Even Bill's nursery sported yellow and mint green curtains and accessories instead of pink and blue. Another plus of his being blond—he always looked clean. Of course, bathing him in his miniature tub gave me so much pleasure that he glowed being immaculate and shiny and smelling of baby powder and lotion. What a good baby! After the first few days he slept through the night only waking at 4 or 5 in the morning. All night TV had just arrived, and I remember watching Humphrey Bogart and other former bright lights perform for me as I fed my child and attempted to stay awake.

During the day walking him in his new gold colored baby buggy constituted a fulfillment of a childhood dream formed when my friend Bubbles and I wheeled our doll carriages on Ocean Parkway's walking path in Brooklyn, calling each other 'Sister'. I wished our doll carriages could match the splendor of the carriages pushed by the grown-up mothers carrying live babies. Now here I walked, pushing my blond infant son in his handsome carriage. Actually, most of my friends owned fancy strollers, as baby buggies of the kind my heart had always been set upon existed more in my memory than in reality because since everyone drove everywhere car seats and the aforementioned folding strollers had replaced them. However, my mother and I had managed to find a soft, foldable, golden colored carriage pretty enough to fulfill my childhood dreams. He possessed a January birthday, but the doctor said he could go outside for walks as soon as he weighed ten pounds as the bracing air would work miracles for his health. Within a short time after his birth he reached the required ten pounds, and walking him around the town where we lived became part of my daily routine. He fell asleep as soon as the cold air and the motion of the carriage combined to lull him. I felt proud of all the admiring comments he received when people peeked into the carriage to look.

Being the first child of his generation in my large family. Bill received oodles of love from my mother and father, sibling, and numerous cousins, uncles and aunts not to mention Harry's family. He even became the object of a great grandmother's adoration. His Christening Party delighted me so much that I saved the pictures of him among my dear friends and family as I opened gifts and rejoiced. My father and I bonded even closer when Bill arrived, and my father worshiped at Bill's altar thinking this child of mine perfect. He took to popping over each Sunday morning after he'd dropped Mother off at church bearing the New York Times and a candy offering for us whether M & M's or a couple of Snickers bars purchased when he bought the paper. The three of us and Bill in his infant seat were lounging together with the TV droning in the background t he Sunday morning when Jack Ruby shot Lee Harvey Oswald. Like the rest of America we'd kept our TV blaring since the moment we'd learned that Jack Kennedy had been shot.

"My God!" my father shouted, "He shot the assassin!" Once again our eyes became riveted upon the history unfolding before us.

My father approved of Bill so much that he took him as a two-year old toddler to a business lunch with his colleagues to my delight and amusement. For if any child embraced the terrible two's Bill did. In fact the terrible two's lasted longer than I like to remember. I often told my husband, "It's a good thing God makes two-year olds so adorable. I approach him harboring anger at his antics in my heart, take one look at his darling face and end up laughing and hugging him."

Nursery school started an unending drama in our lives as Bill got kicked out of nursery school after only three weeks. I'd chosen an exclusive nursery school with taxi service to completely free my mornings. When the head-mistress of this school called to inform us of his expulsion she said, "He's bright and alert, but you'll have problems schooling him. This morning he decided to get down on all fours and bark like a dog just because today's story featured dogs." I settled for a less

exclusive school that accepted him instantly. The woman who ran this second nursery school laughed when she heard my story of his disgrace and said, "We accept any number of Miss McGiffen's drop-outs." However, Miss McGiffen turned out to be a prophet. Bill continued having problems in school although all his teachers agreed that he possessed above average intelligence. His teachers seemed to enjoy his antics, but he disrupted the classes. The school psychologist diagnosed him as border-line hyperactive which I feel his being an only child intensified. I generally dropped everything when he had a question.

When Bill reached the age of seven my father died suddenly of a heart attack. My husband picked me up at the Church where I'd just finished teaching my first grade Sunday School class. I had no idea of anything amiss until we reached home and I spotted Bill kneeling and praying in the front yard. "Harry, what on earth is Bill doing? He appears to be praying outside." I don't remember Harry's words as he broke the news to me of my father's death, but Bill's stricken little face remains etched on my heart. Somehow my child's grief helped me to bear my own. My father left his record collection, heavy with big band era music, to Bill starting for him a life-long love of music especially pre-fifties music. When still a child Bill began clamoring for old fashioned record players. Naturally, we indulged his wishes with the happy result that by the age of thirty-seven he'd amassed a valuable collection of record players and records, most of which he'd paid for himself. His collection contains Edison and RCA record players and numerous old records including a vast group of wax cylinder records all of which I plan to find a home for in the Thomas Edison Museum in West Orange New Jersey under Bill's name.

Being an only child Bill brought his array of friends home often. Even when he began to date seriously he brought the girls over for dinner without my asking. He appeared to be proud of his father and me—what a compliment. When in college he seemed delighted when we visited the campus and would introduce us happily to the Deans. Although Bill hated high school he couldn't get enough of college. He attended Seton Hall and received a Bachelor's degree and then a Master's degree. He later went to Drew University in Madison New Jersey where he obtained at least one more Master's Degree and his Doctorate. He ended up with a Master's in History and Psychology, a Master's of Philosophy, and a Doctorate in History. Miss McGiffin finally proved wrong! Two years ago Bill achieved his goal—a tenure track position at a college in New York State and the hope of buying a Tudor style house.

On August 20, 2000 Bill visited Harry and me for the weekend. After dining at our favorite Japanese restaurant the three of us headed for home. As we stopped for a light heedless of approaching danger, an RV whose driver saw the light change but neglected to spot our car sitting there about to drive away rammed into us killing Bill instantly and critically injuring my Harry. Thank God, Harry who is mending arrived home for Thanksgiving and will be home for Christmas. We are trying to understand why Bill had to leave us. He leaves behind a legacy of love. Love he gave to us and to all who knew him especially the young people he taught. The college where he taught held a memorial service outside on the campus, and the students clustered and sat wherever they could find an available space. I have to believe he is with my father now, and that we will see them both someday.

A TRAIN RIDE
WITH DADDY

If Billy hadn't begun wheezing signifying the start of an asthma attack, the whole family would have boarded the train together. However, since her Dad had only two weeks vacation he decided to ride the train to Maine first with Suzette, and Suzette's Mother and Billy could follow in a day or so. Suzette felt a combination of delight and apprehension regarding this development for although she worshiped her father she also feared his fierce temper. He seemed a mystery figure as he worked long hours, and Suzette seldom saw him. When they reached Grand Central Station she had little time to wonder about anything as she absorbed herself in the sights and sounds surrounding her.

Her Dad excused himself leaving Suzette sitting on a bench and quickly returned carrying a brown bag that he presented to her. " A gift for you," he said smiling.

"Oh, can I open it?"

"Please do."

Suzette reached inside the bag and grabbed not one but two wrapped parcels. She tore open the paper on the first one she grabbed and cooed when she saw a basket of fluffy kittens who looked real and felt silky. She hated to put the kittens down long enough to open the second package that contained a box filled with color books, dot books and puzzle books accompanied by a large box of crayons.

"To work with on the train," her Dad said.

"Daddy, you remembered how much I like coloring."

Although Dad grunted his response, Suzette felt contented as they boarded the train and she squealed her happiness when he gave her the window seat. When the train finally groaned and chugged to signal its starting, she struggled to contain her excitement. Between looking out the window at the moving scenery and changing landscapes and coloring in her new books the ride whizzed by as fast as the train. Before she could believe it Dad signaled that they should head for the dining car for lunch. Suzette thought the dining car cunning, and fascinated she chose a table close to the window. She noticed an old woman and a child wearing glasses and a Lord Fauntleroy suit seated at the table next to them. Something about the pair fascinated Suzette, and she pointed them out to her Dad surreptitiously. "Look, Daddy, she whispered, the lady is wearing a pincenez."

Dad smiled and said, "Yes she is and fancy your knowing that word."

Now Suzette glowed from having pleased her Dad. She read all she could get hold of and did know numerous big words. She peeked at the dignified woman and the boy and observed that the boy glared at her as if she'd done something wrong. She didn't have long to wait to find out the problem. The boy leaned toward the woman and stage whispered, "Grandma, that little girl said that you stink."

The old lady appeared shocked and wasted no time expressing her outrage to Suzette's Dad. "Sir, your daughter insulted me. What a crude thing for her to say."

"Madam," Dad said, "my daughter merely commented on your glasses. She even knew that they are called pincenez glasses, and said so. Actually, I'm proud of her vocabulary. If anyone got out of line, I'd choose your grandson. He either misunderstood or tried to cause trouble."

As the old woman bristled at her Dad's words, Suzette said, "I don't think your grandson meant to upset us all. Maybe he and I could sit together for part of the ride?"

Suzette's words turned the tables, and everyone laughed. She felt rich with her father's approval and generous enough to try to befriend the hapless boy. She knew that she and her Dad would laugh for years over this contretemps. The rest of the trip to Maine sped by, and she hugged the lunchtime incident to her heart loving how her Dad had leapt to her defense like a Knight in Shining Armor.

ROY

What an original Maggie Sue thought whenever she pondered Roy. He directed shows along with Mr. Deeds for the Drama Class and the Drama Club. He acted in some of the plays too, but even directed in the plays in which he acted. His intelligence soared so high that he skipped senior year and went directly to Princeton at the end of his junior year without graduating. His parents gave him a red Jaguar that he drove to high school every day and parked along with the bikes of his fellow students and the occasional beat up job driven by one of the luckier kids. He spoke with an English upper class accent and excelled in chess. He and his closest friend Dennis stuck together as if glued with Krazy glue. Dennis shared Roy's brightness, but had neither the money nor the aloof attitude Roy seemed to possess without realizing he did.

"Do you think Roy and Dennis are a couple?" Maggie Sue asked Maryann sotto voce enjoying the thrill of the forbidden thought regarding something about which she knew less than nothing.

"Who knows," Maryann responded. "They deserve their privacy. It's not as if they flaunt their special relationship. Roy dates sometimes, and Dennis asked you out after the last Drama Club production."

"Yeah, but that's different. The whole cast falls in like after a show," Maggie Sue said.

None the less, Maggie Sue found Roy intriguing. During the runs of the plays in which she starred, she trailed after him needing his opinion and advice regarding her performance. He always gave her good suggestions. Once when he chose the actors for the newest play the Drama Club produced he chose her for the part she coveted before he chose any other actor. Maggie Sue found Dennis easier to talk to, and the two of them hit it off during the plays in which they appeared together. Maggie Sue thought of a date with Dennis like having a coke with a friend, and indeed their dates as such consisted of cokes after school at the local sweet shop. She held curiosity about dating Roy as he'd not as yet asked her out. She wanted to ride in the red Jaguar. In the summer of their junior year just before he left for Princeton Roy invited Maggie Sue to go to the movies with him and his Jaguar.

What a steamy night. Almost sultry. The ride to the movie theater in the Jaguar fulfilled all Maggie Sue's expectations about the neat car. Roy appeared shocked and fascinated when Maggie Sue lit a cigarette.

"Wow, you're the first girl I ever dated who smokes," he trilled. "The movie we're about to see has an appropriate name for tonight, doesn't it?"

"The Long Hot Summer" has to be great with Paul Newman and his ice blue eyes and Joanne Woodward starring in it."

After the movie on the way to Maggie Sue' s house driving through the hot night only barely cooled by the breeze of the convertible top Roy pronounced, "It surely was "The Long Hot Summer" wasn't it? You could feel the heat generated by the two of them."

"I guess you could. Photoplay said they fell in love making this movie. You call that explosion between them chemistry," Maggie Sue replied.

Roy kissed her goodnight still sitting in the Jag, but he declined her invitation to come in for some lemonade. Maggie Sue couldn't read his feelings for her. She instinctively felt that he had surface feelings for her, and she intuited that she didn't turn him on regardless of his sexy comments. Maybe this remained a mystery even to Roy. When September arrived Maggie Sue guessed she'd seen the last of Roy. She had no time to think about him, however, as in her senior year she dated a college senior from the local college. Maggie Sue invited this Kevin and Maryann took Pete his fraternity brother and Maryann's steady to the all school production of "The King and I." In the lobby of the high school during intermission Maggie Sue bumped smack into Roy. Roy seemed anxious to meet Kevin and Pete and said in his upper crust accent, "Hi, I attend Princeton. What University do you chaps attend?"

However Kevin and Pete seemed to treat this as a question needing no reply and gave none. Soon Roy drifted out of Maggie Sue's horizon for the last time. Many times thereafter the foursome laughed over the hapless Roy' s exchange with the boys about colleges. Kevin often mimicked Roy's accent producing helpless laughter from Maggie Sue. However, when she looked back over her years in drama and adventures with the Drama Club she remembered Roy. She never changed her mind about his being an original.

RAY & ESTELLE

Ray appeared shocked, stunned by the kiss Maggie and Kevin shared at midnight on New Year's Eve. Kevin later told Maggie that he'd said "Kevin, watch this one. She's wild. A tiger cub."

Granted, Maggie thought, New Year's Eve might count as a first date, but even strangers kissed welcoming in the New Year without inciting criticism. Her first meeting with Kevin shot off a shower of sparks exploding into fireworks when Kevin's lips touched Maggie's. Maggie learned early in her dating life with Kevin that this brooding, rugged, rough-edged friend. Ray, loomed large in Kevin's life and henceforth in hers. Ray, in Maggie's opinion a lone cowboy, had just returned from a trip to Texas and Mexico. He bragged of his adventures constantly causing Kevin to grin and say, "Ask him about his encounter with the Mexican lady of the evening who read comic books avidly."

However to Maggie the street walker and her comics remained a mystery for eternity, along with references alluded to by Ray's calling Kevin 'Stick', a laughter generated by the two friends regarding their bonding over "The Untouchables" each Thursday evening. Ray's initial disapproval of Maggie soon turned into what looked to Maggie like a paternal fondness shown by Ray toward her. If Kevin and Ray formed part of a club completed by a third friend from both their high school and college days named Pete, the clubhouse where they met was Gene's Tavern near the college. Here the guys, their girls, and an assortment of Upsala's fraternity brothers and sorority sisters gathered nightly. Maggie drank oodles of cokes while the guys gulped beer. The smoky tavern held a jukebox featuring Johnny Mathias make-out music and a back room for card playing and pool.

"Kevin's Valentine card was this big," Maggie giggled and stretched out her hands giving sway to a volley of laughs from the boys whose eyes looked as though they contained dirty secrets. Fortunately for Maggie, Kevin's friend Pete dated her closest friend, Maryann. This gave Maggie a constant ally and partner in crime and someone with whom to share the endless cokes. Maggie worried about Ray as he seemed to be dateless much of the time. Maggie didn't mind his tagging along on hers and Kevin's dates, but she wanted him to join the fun. Also Maggie enjoyed matchmaking. The protectiveness Ray showed Maggie continued when one Saturday afternoon he insisted on taking her along with Kevin to his house to meet his family. Kevin already considered Ray's family's his second home, and he seemed pleased that Ray wanted to make these introductions.

"An Italian girl," Ray's mother crooned. "Look, Papa, Kevin's dating an Italian girl. Raymond, why don't you bring home an Italian girl like this one."

Maggie smiled. Being Italian had never seemed so desirable before. Now she preened enjoying the attention Ray's folks lavished on her. Kevin grinned looking proud, and Maggie thanked Ray inwardly for being the source of her being seen in such golden rays of light. In return for his watching over her, Maggie arranged endless blind dates for Ray with good friends

and even cousins of hers. Unfortunately none panned out, and once a crisis occurred when Ray fell hard for one of Maggie's cousins who didn't return the favor. When Kevin went away for his annual trek to National Guard Camp he requested that Ray look after Maggie. Ray did so with such enthusiasm that it prompted Kevin's mother to tease Maggie about Ray's having a crush on her. "No," Maggie demurred, "Ray loves us as a couple. It's our romance he envies."

However, for whatever reason Ray guarded Maggie, she basked in the warmth of his caring. Ray enlivened the long two weeks that Kevin attended National Guard Camp by arriving on her doorstep one Saturday night, sharing a meatloaf dinner with her family and taking her to see Disney's "Sleeping Beauty." After the movie ended she and Ray sat companionably on her sofa in the TV room watching "Bride of Frankenstein." Kevin's mother could tease all she wished, Maggie knew that Kevin didn't believe Ray had a crush on her anymore than she did. The search to find Ray a girl of his own continued with Maggie's calling on Maryann to help.

When Ray finally fell in love he did it without the interference of either Maggie or Maryann. He met an aloof, mature, attractive woman named Estelle who owned her own hairdressers' shop. Maryann who seemed delighted that Estelle did hair, initiated weekly trips for herself and Maggie to Estelle's shop. The three girls bonded quickly, and although Estelle sometimes complained about Maryann's being a snob to Maggie she appeared to be pleased that the girls patronized her shop. One time, again when Kevin vanished to Camp Drum for two weeks, Estelle gave Maggie a red rinse causing Kevin to freak until he saw Maggie and realized it only gave highlights to what she considered her abundant black hair. The three couples went bowling, to the movies, and became engaged. Maggie's and Kevin's wedding happened first followed by Maryann's and Pete's. Estelle seemed to fret about how long Ray claimed to want to save money before their marriage, but soon appeared to glow with anticipation when the couple set a date.

"Blue. I want my new apartment furnished in blue—sofas, curtains, carpets, etc. If I could walk down the aisle in blue, too, I would."

Maggie confided to Maryann, "I've never seen anyone as thrilled with the prospect of marriage as Estelle. She seems so sure of herself."

Maggie experienced disappointment over Estelle's and Ray's asking Maryann and Pete to stand up with them at their wedding rather than Kevin and Maggie. "Estelle has always confided in me. She even dished Maryann. Why didn't they ask us?"

"Maggie, Ray and Pete were the close ones in high school. My friendship with Ray came in college. Pete is the older friend."

"I think Estelle is jealous of Maggie," stated Kevin's mother.

"He must have made the mistake of confiding in her about how he used to feel about Maggie."

"Mom, that's ridiculous," Maggie countered.

Whatever the reason, Kevin refused to allow this to mar the friendship, and he looked forward to the wedding. Estelle's happiness threatened to overflow and spill on to everyone with whom she came in contact. Never had Maggie seen such an eager bride. Estelle shared each detail of the preparations with Maggie and Maryann. Maggie listened patiently trying not to show boredom no matter how many times she heard the plans for the wedding and reception repeated. She began to feel as familiar with the decor of Ray's and Estelle's apartment as with her own.

The glory day arrived, and Maggie wearing blue chiffon from head to foot entered the Church with Kevin. Maryann looked gorgeous as she walked calmly and elegantly down the long aisle—chosen for its length. Then came Estelle on her father's arm. Maggie craned her neck for a look at Estelle in her finery, and to her surprise Estelle wobbled and cried her way down the seemingly endless aisle. "I don't believe this, Kevin. She's always so confident and polished. She'd anticipated this day for so long, and now she sheds tears all the way to the altar."

"I don't understand the way you women think anyway, Maggie. Don't look to me for answers."

After the tears sunshine reigned, and the rest of the ceremony and the reception held in the Church's reception area shone. Now Ray and Estelle formed a couple. No longer could Maggie think of Ray as the Lone Ranger. Although rationally she knew she'd gained a friend in

Estelle and didn't lose one in Ray, emotionally she felt as though a limb had been severed. For so long Kevin, Ray, and she had combined together into a threesome. Marriage changed all three couples' friendship, and now they shared life-changing events with each other—new homes, jobs and babies. Maggie agreed with Thomas Wolfe you can't go home again. Thank goodness youth can be remembered always just by pushing memory's buttons.

BLACK SWEAT SHIRTS

Afterwards she wondered how she'd misread the signs. Maybe because she felt happy with him and thought he'd changed her life. Maybe because she believed she knew the real Phil behind the bluff. Maybe just because he represented her first love. Anyhow they rocked together whenever Mark vanished. For Mark's constant presence threatened to upset their romance. When Gail met Phil he and Mark came together as a package. She could enjoy Phil's company if she were willing to allow Mark along wherever they went. Every once in a bit, her presence created ripples in the twosome's friendship, and for a while Mark disappeared.

"Why does your tightness with Mark have to affect our relationship?"

"Gail, you don't understand. Before Mark I stood alone. Other guys threw pizza at me. Mark and I started the Black Sweat Shirts."

"So now they throw pizza at your whole group."

But Gail understood what Phil meant and why his friendship with Mark mattered. She, too, had felt ostracized by the preppies and the jocks as she dressed in black and emulated the Beatniks of old. She troubled over the standards their high school espoused, but she'd read enough to know that college held aloft brighter hopes because of more areas to shine. She knew that someday she'd find friends to share her interests in literature and creative writing even if not here at the high school. She thought Phil looked rugged and handsome, thought his brooding showed his deepness, and even found Mark interesting looking. She worried about Phil's preoccupation with the jocks' slights, but thought maybe boys minded being left out of the loop more than girls did.

"Does it help, Phil, to join forces with other people the rest deride and call losers?"

"Yes because at least we bolster each other and together possess more physical strength than we would alone."

"So you feel that a gang composed of nerds and geeks helps more than standing by yourself? Personally, I take pride in my difference from the preppies. I enjoy holding myself away from the crowd. I could attempt to dress correctly and meet their standards, but I choose looking different."

"I know, Gail, and your strength and character drew me to you in the first place."

Since Phil's final answer pleased her, Gail dropped the subject. She still puzzled over his preoccupation with the computer and Mark, but she knew that computers occupied most teens' time and used up their drive. She attempted savoring the time Phil allotted to her and not pester him with questions. After all, she liked him, and maybe his oddness had drawn her to him in the first place. She enjoyed his company, reveled in his intelligence, and purred when they kissed. As much as she delighted in Phil when he and Mark temporarily split, she learned more about Phil when Mark accompanied them. During one of their threesome dates, Gail overheard the two boys engaging in a charged discussion about guns. As they argued or sometimes debated the virtues of one kind of firearm over another she shivered. Did all boys like guns? She herself feared guns and felt glad that her father possessed no weapons. Gail supported Rosie O'Donnell regarding gun control. Maybe the love of guns and war movies accompanied the territory boys occupied. She fell silent and eavesdropped on their conversation pretending she wool gathered. When Mark said, "Phil, let's go to that gun show in Dover next Saturday," she perked up.

"Why would anyone want to go to a gun show? Are you planning on buying guns?" she asked.

"Calm down, Gail. Of course Mark and I won't buy guns. We like browsing and fantasizing about guns."

"Fantasizing how. About using them? On whom?"

"Come on, Gail. Haven't you every dreamed of getting back at the snobby girls in the school?' Phil asked.

"My only dream of revenge is succeeding and coming back famous. I've never wished harm to anyone even in my daydreams."

"Computer games destroy enemies. How is our fantasy different?" Phil's words sounded fevered, and his eyes glazed.

"It just is. Computer games and movies are fake."

Sensing that Phil's mood had darkened, Gail switched the subject, and soon the three headed out for hamburgers. But, she trembled inwardly and felt queasy about the conversation. Again, she wondered whether boys harbored violent thoughts more than girls did. The macho posturing. Phil never mentioned the gun show again. As spring approached Gail's thoughts turned to the Junior Prom's coming up. She knew that Mark not only didn't have a girlfriend to take but harbored no crush on anyone. Would Phil escort her to the Prom if Mark remained at home? She didn't have long to wait. A month before the Prom Phil approached her after the math class they shared.

"Gail, let's go to the Prom. A bunch of the Sweat Shirts are going. We'll have our own table."

"But, what about Mark?"

"He's cool. Well maybe not, but I want to go."

Gail took the invitation as a sign that her fears might be silly. Would Phil go to the Prom if he hated the world? Would Phil risk Mark's anger if Mark's influence ruled him? Gail thought that Mark's disenchantment with people ran deeper than Phil's did. Each break in the boys' friendship bolstered her hope that she and Phil could escape from Mark's power. As the weeks before the Prom melted away Gail's suspicions faded and then disappeared as she chose her dress, planned her hairdo, and whispered the color of her dress to Phil. Phil told her he'd wear a black tuxedo.

"Following tradition, or to go along with the Sweat Shirt theme?" she asked.

"Both," he answered grinning.

Mark glared at her during the time before the Prom, but appeared to hold his feelings to himself at least verbally. If he assaulted Phil with his anger, Gail heard nothing about it. Prom night glowed. Even sitting at the losers' table worked for Gail as she took the time to meet the other boys and their girlfriends and found them shy but nice. Gail enjoyed her romance that night and began looking forward to spending the summer with Phil minus Mark. She stayed in the dark regarding the coming event that would change her life and the life of all those around her. The warm late spring days enveloped her and accented the drowse and contentment she'd fallen into. By the time June arrived Phil's friendship with Mark appeared to be close again, but Gail, remembering the Prom, stopped worrying about it. She really had no right to interfere with Phil's closeness to Mark as long as Phil gave date time to her. Also Phil told her that Mark and his family planned a trip to their lake house for the entire month of July.

When the first shots pierced the stillness of the languid afternoon Gail thought some car had backfired. Seconds later she heard screams that chilled her and made a lurch of fear dart through her body. Following the screams she saw sobbing incoherent teens running through the halls and out the nearest exit. She and others sitting in the classroom dashed to the door of the classroom and someone yelled, "What's happening? Were those shots?"

"Run," one of the rushing teens gasped. "They've got guns and they're shooting everyone in sight."

Gail's teacher took charge and herded the roomful of teens into a semblance of order. "Walk as though for a fire drill, and head for the nearest exit," she ordered. "Don't panic."

Panic, however, filled the room, and the group of teens tore through the door and the confused halls, and propelled themselves toward the exit. Gail heard Phil's and Mark's names as she galloped down the hall. No she thought. It couldn't be they. If any one were on a gun rampage it would have to be intruders, gangsters, thieves. Why would Phil and Mark turn guns on anyone? She must have heard wrong. When she finally reached the relative safety of the school's lawn, she wondered no longer as a girl from her home room pointed to her yelling, "It's your Phil and his creepy friend. They are armed and shooting. Laughing as they shoot and taunting the kids in range. It's your freaky friends." The girl seemed to dissolve as she spoke and turned away crying. Most of the girls clung to each other sobbing, and even the boys appeared to be shaking with tears and fright.

Shock, fear and nausea gripped Gail. The guilt would come later. She caught a quick thought of trying to find Phil and attempting to stop the carnage and madness. How could her Phil have snapped? He'd have to be crazy to want to kill people let alone actually do it. How could such an intelligent guy even consider murder? Even in her mixed-up state she couldn't excuse his actions by knowing that Mark must have instigated the whole thing. She realized she had to try and reach him before anyone else died. "Where," she choked out," are the boys shooting? I'll go and plead with them to stop."

"They were shooting in the cafeteria the last I heard," the girl who'd accused her said. "Going after them and cutting off any more killing is the least you could do, you sleaze."

Ignoring the insult Gail hurled herself toward the school's side door nearest the cafeteria. As soon as her hand touched the door a teacher grabbed her and pulled her back into the yard.

"Those boys are beyond reaching at this point. We can't let you risk your own life."

As Gail sobbed with fright and frustration the students continued to pour out of the building screaming and crying. She could hear further shots and shrieking. She trembled with feelings she'd never experienced before. Now the guilt hit. She couldn't feel more wrenching guilt if she'd wielded the guns herself. Reports of the dead and injured rang out around her. No one knew for sure how many people had died or been hurt, and when the police arrived the bedlam deepened. The police seemed unsure as to how to proceed and hesitated before entering the school even with their own weapons. Just when Gail thought she'd experienced the worst pain she could stand a new rumor surfaced.

"Those two worms shot themselves. Laughing while they murdered others, they laughed while they shot themselves," someone reported.

Hoping she'd heard wrong or that the report would prove wrong, Gail started praying. Praying for the dead and wounded kids, praying for Phil and even Mark and praying to have the strength to go on another moment in this world. As reports of the death toll increased, Gail stood alone while the other kids grasped each other for support. Anxious parents began showing up at the school looking near hysteria as they searched for their children. Finally Gail spotted her mother at the edge of the crowd craning her neck and calling Gail's name in a frantic voice.

Gail dashed toward her, throwing her arms around her and letting her stroke and hug her. She only knew that now she could let go.

"It was Phil and Mark. They went berserk. I never knew. Oh, God."

"Hush, Gail, we'll go home now. Somehow Daddy and I will get you through this."

But Gail's guilt and agony increased in the week that followed. Word of the boys' having collected an arsenal of weapons shook her. How could she have been so obtuse? Did she blind herself to something she should have guessed? Some of the other boys in the Black Sweat Shirts chilled her when they told her that Mark and sometimes Phil had confided in them that they wanted revenge and planned a massacre.

"Why didn't you tell me, at least?" she kept repeating. But she knew she mightn't have listened or believed either. Knowing that she shared her own guilt with the other boys in the gang didn't assuage her. Even if she could stop hating herself, the other students in the high school mocked her throwing savage words her way at every turn. Her parents too told her that the scorn shown them defied belief. Too, her parents seemed to absorb the guilt she bore. Shame followed for Gail. She felt compassion for the school's loss—the deaths of so many classmates. But the others could share their grief. Take comfort in pain borne together. She couldn't even attend the victim's funerals. She didn't dare. She suffered alone and her burning shame caused her to believe she deserved the abuse heaped upon her. She pleaded with her parents to send her away or to move to another state where her name wasn't a dirty word. One day her parents told her that for her sake, the sake of her younger sister, and for their own peace of mind they would relocate as Gail's father had obtained a transfer.

"Gail, this will be a fresh start for you. No one will have to know," her mother said.

But Gail needed to take something from this experience. She searched her mind trying to learn where she'd slipped up. What should she have done? What could she do differently the next time? Maybe she would have to keep herself from losing perspective by letting romance blur her clarity. Had she even known Phil? If she had she'd never have loved him. Had she been in love with a cardboard figure she'd fashioned from her own needs? Knowing that Phil's and Mark's parents suffered far more than she and her family, she forced herself to visit each set of parents offering them the only words of sympathy she knew they'd received. If she could forgive them before moving on, maybe she could find a way to forgive herself. She hoped that she now could be a positive influence on other people the way she should have and wanted to influence Phil. No romance would be better than a romance only in her mind. She'd survive even this, but her trust and faith in the human situation had been shaken as if by an earthquake. Like the survivors of an earthquake she couldn't even take the ground she stood on for granted.

STEWART WALKS
SALLY HOME

Even though just a third grader Sally knew Stewart fell into the Nerd category. He wore thick glasses and told everyone that he had one blind eye. This awoke curiosity among the rest of the third graders. How could you see with just one eye? What would the world look like askew? Besides being blind, Stewart ranked at the top of the class in brains, and he actually had a pocket protector in his shirt pocket behind the ballpoint pens. Stewart also had one sweet smile. Lately, Sally noticed that his smiles seemed to beam toward her as if with laser. He followed her about in the classroom too and in the playground at recess. Already her friends had started to tease Sally about Stewart's obvious crush. One Friday afternoon as she walked home, Sally noticed that Stewart had fallen in step with her.

"Here, give me your books. I'll be glad to carry them along with mine," he said smiling.

"Stewart, I can carry my own books. Girls are not weaker," Sally said. But she soon felt stricken with an attack of conscience and added, "But thank you for asking."

She realized that this last constituted an assent on her part, as he showed no signs of leaving her side. She knew that he lived in the other part of town so there seemed to be no way to toss this off as coincidence. He looked so happy to be right here with her. Like all his dreams had been realized. For the first time Sally knew what it felt like to have someone else's happiness depending on what she did or said. She tasted this power, and wondered how she felt about it. When they arrived at her door Sally automatically said, "Do you want to come in for a coke?"

"You mean it, Sally? I sure do."

Sally's mother being of the cool variety as mothers go in Sally's opinion, welcomed Stewart with aplomb and behaved as though Sally's having boys over for a coke were the norm. Sally surprised herself by behaving as calmly as though her guest came over every afternoon. She also surprised herself by enjoying his company. Who would have expected Stewart to have a knife point sharp wit and to have such a sarcastic view of his classmates and even himself and his shortcomings. She discovered that Stewart's jokes about his mother simultaneously rang true and carried a hint of trouble bubbling beneath the surface of the laughter. In Sally's experience no mother could be so severe and stern.

"When she barks orders, I jump," he joked.

One day after school when Stewart placed himself beside Sally as usual he queried, "How'd you like to walk to town for a coke. I'll walk you home after."

During the walk Stewart confided that his mother had told him she disapproved of his relationship with Sally. She'd forbidden him to continue walking her home.

"Stewart, what on earth are you doing with me now?" "She said not to walk you home. She didn't say anything about going to the Sweet Shop for a coke. Besides, she's working at O'Grady's Dress Shop now." He looked somewhat chagrined and sheepish at the finish of his bravely begun statement. "Stewart, I totally understand if you stay away from me. I don't want to be the cause of any trouble between you and your mother." Privately, she thought this would end the Stewart problem as well as help him as she had begun to care about him as a friend.

Sally and Stewart enjoyed a coke at the Sweet Shop and were almost to Sally's house when Stewart spied his mother's car driving a short way behind them on the street. "Darn," he said. "I'm grounded or worse for sure."

Sally never saw Stewart again. It must have been a case of "or worse." The school grapevine reported that Stewart enrolled at the Hun private school for boys and actually boarded there coming home only for weekends. Sally knew that he would remember her as an expensive extra he could have done without. She hoped that the time away at boarding school would strengthen him in his future forays with his witch of a mother.

THE LIBRARY

Jenny loved reading books. She'd been reading books since she'd been taught how to read by her Aunt Phyllis. Her cousin Andy, two years older than Jenny, advised her on her reading fare. When Andy cried, "Jenny, put away THE BOBBSEY TWINS and B IS FOR BETSY and read MARY POPPINS," Jenny obeyed instantly. If Andy thought this MARY POPPINS superior to her regular menu. Jenny wanted to try MARY POPPINS.

Even the trip to the library Jenny thought wonderful. The first time she ventured to the library her mother crossed her over the wide Ocean Parkway through the whizzing traffic, but after seeing how well Jenny looked both ways before crossing and followed the traffic light, her mother allowed her to set forth alone. After the scary crossing, Jenny passed the cleaner's shop where Hitler hanged in effigy. Next Jenny averted her eyes while passing the chicken slaughterhouse with its smells and sights of blood. Sometimes when she approached the chicken slaughterhouse she'd cross the street to avoid passing it.

But arriving at her goal—the library— seemed worth all the dangers averted. The sight and the smell of the books transfixed Jenny. Just looking at the bounty arrayed in front of her made her dizzy with the longing to read all the tomes.

After choosing her books, she'd sniff them and hold them close to her while walking home. If she should happen to find a sequel to a favorite book, she'd kiss the book during the homeward walk. Sometimes the books distracted her on her walk home and she might be less careful crossing Ocean Parkway than she'd been on the way to the library. On the day she borrowed MARY POPPINS from the library after Andy enticed her into discarding her baby books in favor of this one she made the mistake of delving into the book before leaving the library. Mistake because she got hooked and her mind stayed in London with the rosy complexioned Mary and her mischief making charges while her feet headed toward Ocean Parkway. When her feet along with her dragging and reluctant mind reached the busy intersection her eyes registered the sight of horseback riders on the walking path. The horses trotted briskly, and one horse dropped a horse chestnut as he passed her path of vision. Jenny began crossing the street after the horse clumped by without checking the light or looking both ways up and down the street. "Hey, girlie, that's how they make angels," an irate man shouted out the widow, and Jenny awoke from her book and horse induced trance realizing that the light glared red from the traffic post. A hot, sick feeling pierced her chest, and she backtracked to the curb.

Reading often caused her to lose track of time and place. Her household held turbulence due to battling parents who exhibited tantrums and tempers. Reading transported her to peaceful parks, cool ocean beaches, and picture perfect families containing dimpled children and calm parents. Reading's escape suited Jenny to perfection. Although Andy's family life seemed calm to Jenny, she told Jenny "Reading takes me on adventures where I learn about other lives and locales."

Although Andy and Jenny lived in the same two-family house when Jenny learned to read and through her first three reading years. Jenny and her family moved from Brooklyn to New Jersey during Jenny's seventh year. Jenny's new house contained a library filled with books written for teenage girls. Here Jenny could get her fill of Nancy Drew and a new mystery solver named Judy Bolton, who unlike Nancy Drew, grew older as the series of books unfolded. Here Jenny discovered books about career girls, and old-fashioned books that took place before women had the vote. Until she tumbled upon these books. Jenny never realized that a time existed when women couldn't vote. The first summer Jenny lived in the house with the book-filled library Andy came to visit. She and Andy spent one whole week outside on the screened in porch reading the books. They each carried down a handful each morning and returned the finished books to the library each evening. For once Jenny's mother didn't interrupt to say, "Stop reading. Go outside, get some sun and exercise. Go play tennis in the park." Not with Andy here.

However, before her visit ended Andy embarked on some mischief that scared Jenny as Andy had intended. On the day before the visit came to a close Jenny discovered that she'd forgotten to return an overdue library book and asked Andy if she'd like to walk to the library with her to return it.

"How overdue is the book?" Andy inquired.

"Gee, it looks like two weeks," Jenny said sounding fretful.

"Two weeks. Books later than one week require the attention of the Library Police. A fearsome crew!"

"Andy, what on earth are the Library Police?"

"The Library Police are giant sized fellows, far more fearsome than policemen on the beat, who punish people with overdue fines."

"But, Andy, why haven't I ever seen or heard of them?"

"They reside in a secret room in the library where they bring you if your book is later than a week. Once in the secret room nobody knows what they do. I've heard that it's terrible whatever tortures they inflict."

"Should I throw the book away and never enter the library again?"

"No, they have ways and methods of catching you. The library keeps records of who has its books. You know that. But, Jenny, I'll go with you and lend whatever support I'm allowed to give. Let's go. I feel like going into town anyway."

Andy's offer to accompany her cheered Jenny somewhat, but her terror rose and increased with each step leading her closer to the library. On one level she couldn't believe that a place she loved as much as her library could pose any kind of a threat. Rather, the library provided her with pleasures beyond counting. But, Jenny believed and trusted Andy and right now she'd forgotten all the pranks

Andy had played on her before. Holding on to Andy's hand she entered the library and presented her book at the desk, limbs trembling and hands shaking.

"Hi, Jenny. Did you like the new MARY POPPINS IN THE PARK? You owe the library 50 cents, and we need the money."

Relief flooded through her body and Jenny gladly surrendered 50 cents from her allowance. She felt too happy to be angry with Andy. Rather she puzzled over her continued gullibility. Yes, her instincts of good vibes regarding the library held fast. Libraries and bookstores holding their treasures would always attract Jenny. Books contained the power to teach and entertain, and as long as a book lay within reach. Jenny knew she always had company.

FELIX THE CAT

"... The wonderful, wonderful cat." The song lyrics certainly described Felix, Tracy and Kevin's first cat, and because of his unique and steadfast qualities the first in a long line of cats forming a dynasty of cats. It came about that Eric wanted a cat and Pixie became pregnant again. Pixie, the Fowler's cat, gave birth about once a year, and this year Eric's friend, Jeff, offered Eric one of the coming litter. How could he refuse this temptation? Tracy knew that Eric had no intention of turning from this temptation and instead she smiled as he shouted news of the event all through the house pleading and easily exacting a promise from her and Kevin that when Pixie gave birth this time, Eric might have the pick of the litter. To further cement the deal, Tracy telephoned Jeff's mother and confirmed the offer discovering that she and Jeff's father would be grateful for Eric's choosing and taking home a kitten. Pixie, their favorite cat of all time, seemed a little too promiscuous for Jeff's parents. Finding homes for the yearly myriad of kittens seemed a bit much. Pixie's being a gray and white Tabby made Tracy think that they'd be getting a Tabby, too, and they thought of Tiger or Tabby as names for the coming event.

The day Pixie gave birth Jeff ran over and invited Eric to come see the new-born kittens. Jeff galloped over to the Fowler's house, and drifted home looking already in love with the lone black and white kitten in the litter. Tracy knew he wanted this kitten. The pick of the litter! Jeff's parents, too, seemed to feel that the black and white kitten was the star. Tracy felt a bit disappointed as she liked Tabby cats, but after all Eric had the option of choosing whatever kitten he wanted, and he wanted the small black and white one. He never wavered from his decision from the first moment he saw the different one in the bunch. Tracy knew that the eight weeks that the new kitten had to stay with Pixie seemed intolerably long for Eric. Coming smack as they did in the middle of the long, hot summer didn't help matters any. Tracy tried all forms of distraction such as trips to the community pool swimming with his pals and taking him shopping for school clothes for his first day of kindergarten coming up quickly upon him. But not even the long-awaited first day of school seemed to unfasten Eric's mind from the kitten. He considered names for days finally coming up triumphantly with Mailbox. Tracy tactfully tried to discourage this appellation for a long while with no results. Eventually, as his favorite show of the year, Felix the Cat, kept blaring out the famous theme song, Eric decided upon Felix to the whole family's resounding approval.

Eric's first day of school came and went, the air started to crisp, the leaves began to flame into red, orange and gold, and the eight weeks that Pixie needed to care for the kittens came to an end. Finally the day arrived when Eric could fetch Felix. At home preparations had been made to welcome the kitten—a food bowl and litter box waited for Felix. Eric who had been allowed to collect Felix alone, thundered into the house holding this little scrap of fur in his arms. Felix looking bewildered scrambled under the hi fi set in the living room and refused to budge. However, Eric, seeming undaunted, began to woo and coax the kitten from where he lay under the Hi-Fi. Eric at first tossed the little catnip mice and rubber balls purchased especially for Felix to him. Seeing that this didn't seem to work, Eric threw his favorite stuffed animals under the hi fi to entice Felix to exit. Finally Eric said,

"Let's try to ignore Felix, and maybe he'll appear.'

Sure enough, long before Kevin came home from work that evening, Felix had integrated himself into the household exploring his new environment. Frequently, he disappeared causing Tracy and Eric to search the house for him. After minutes of fruitless searching either Mother or son would spot his small body curled up on the afghan on the den couch or under a dresser in the bedroom. No spot seemed too remote for Felix to investigate, and he remained alert and friendly letting out with a meow every once in a while which seemed to delight Eric. Eric had sacrificed his huge last year's Easter basket that he'd named Caesar to give to Felix for a bed, and therefore had lined the basket with an old baby blanket of his and placed several of Felix's more portable toys inside Caesar too. However, when bedtime arrived Felix rejected Caesar in favor of sleeping at the foot of Eric's bed which delighted Eric. He went on subsequent nights to curl up either on Eric's bed or at the foot of Tracy and Kevin's bed. He showed signs of being a sensuous cat loving comfort, warmth and love. All of which he received in giant batches. Tracy knew that Eric looked forward to coming home from kindergarten and finding Felix waiting for him. When Eric's Aunt Mary Ellen heard about Felix's arrival in the household, she presented Eric with a book about Felix the Cat and best of all a record with the Felix the Cat song. Each time Eric played the record he would grab Felix from wherever he had placed himself and put him on his lap rocking him until the end of the record. And he never stopped at playing the record once. After a while when Felix heard the Felix the Cat record he would attempt to hide. He, however, never succeeded in this subterfuge. Eric constantly outsmarted the kitten.

Felix exhibited superior intelligence in all cat things, however. He never got wet in the rain having discovered a small overhang under the house that kept him dry no matter how wild the downpour. Felix caught and killed the rats that were plaguing the neighborhood. He made the family's mice disappear never to return. He entertained cat friends who sat and basked in the sun with him on the patio. Once shortly after his arrival at Eric's house. Pixie came over to visit. Felix seemed delighted to see her. However when it became time for her to take her leave she tried to get him to follow her. He did indeed follow her, but when they reached the edge of the lawn, Felix refused to move off the property. Pixie looked sad but resigned to this and never tried to entice him away again after this time. He owned the title of king cat in the neighborhood as none of the other Toms wanted to take him on. One Spring Felix disappeared for a week, and Tracy called the police department every day. After discovering that Felix was an unaltered Tom, the policeman said "Don't call us, we'll call you." Sure enough a week later Felix reappeared unharmed and hungry. Most of all Felix showed tolerance for many things other cats would not have tolerated. A year or so after Felix's entrance into the household a stray dog appeared in the neighborhood and Eric persuaded Tracy and Kevin to give the puppy a trial period. The puppy appeared to have been mistreated, and showed early signs of being neurotic. He devoured everything in sight, learning from the cat how to climb and jump the small child-proof fence designed to keep him in the kitchen, and once over the fence he attacked and ruined the furniture chewing the stuffing out of some, marking the wood on other pieces, and putting permanent chew marks on the chairs. Felix endured all this outwardly showing no complaint. Occasionally he would look at the family sadly or even sometimes with resignation, but he caused no protest. Fido, the dog, would even chew the shingles on the house when he played outside. Finally, when he began to bite people including one neighborhood child, he had to depart. Tracy and Kevin brought him to an animal shelter, and even Eric seemed to understand why. Felix had full run of the house again. But not for long. On their weekly Friday afternoon trip to the library, Eric and Tracy discovered that the librarian had posted a chart on the bulletin board with the object of finding homes for many stray cats who had landed under her care. Mrs. Procter loved cats and adopted as many as her small house would hold. Eric talked Tracy into driving him right there and then to a house in the country where a stray cat had recently given birth to four kittens. The kittens consisted of three females and one male, all of which had already been named by the lady at whose home the stray cat had chosen to give birth. Eric chose the smallest and the prettiest whose name. Georgette, suited her. Once again they had to wait this time for six more weeks before they could come and get Georgette. But coming to get her proved to be the easy part. Georgette didn't want to be gotten. She escaped from the carton before the car doors had slammed and ran back to her mother and her mistress. The will she exhibited never left this stubborn but adorable cat. She had fluffy fur, almost angora, and almost like a long-haired cat's fur, and her body sat low to the ground. Because of all her cottony fur and her short legs Georgette could be taken for fat, but most decidedly she only owned too much fur. An argument raged throughout the house over the question of whether or not Georgette was fat. Kevin and Eric insisted she was, but Tracy remained adamant that she only looked fat because of the thick fur.

When Georgette became nine months old, she got pregnant. Tracy called the vet and received instructions as how to handle the blessed event. Out of her litter of four, two survived. Brilliant, orange marmalade cats whom the family named Kelly and Colleen because of the Irish red. The small one, named Colleen, turned out to be a boy, and the family who adopted him switched his name to Ding as they said they loved him but felt him to be a ding-a-ling. Kelly became a spoiled darling. Both Georgette and Kelly adored Felix who did not reciprocate these feelings. He gave a frustrated look to Tracy and Eric when they'd arrived with Georgette in arms, but Eric and Tracy decided to keep him ignorant of the birth of the kittens as long as possible. Actually they succeeded in the deception for a while until Georgette decided to move the two kittens from under Tracy and Kevin's bed where she'd given birth to the den. As she moved forward toward the den holding Kelly by the scruff of the neck in her mouth, Felix got a gander at the sight. The look of disgust he gave to Tracy when he beheld this vision could have frozen the Sahara. However, the kittens loved Felix as much as Georgette did. They cuddled against his warm body before drifting off to sleep. The only protest Felix allowed himself came in the form of his opening his mouth wide in the direction of whichever kitten happened to be snuggled against him as if he would bite the little head off. Instead he just fell asleep himself as the kittens knew he would.

Kelly displayed so much confidence that he allowed a neighboring family to adopt him for meals. He simply ate double the food. Felix in time became witness to a parade of cats following Georgette. If he hadn't been such a brick of a cat, Tracy doubted that this menagerie would ever have been collected. However, Felix gave such good press to the cat species that the family couldn't seem to get enough of these furry felines. After a car hit and killed Kelly the family adopted Scruffy a stray from a company garage donated to them by a kind neighbor who strove to replace Kelly with another red cat. However when Scruffy arrived he appeared to be a gray cat so dirty did his fur appear. Tiger, and Christie Love followed Scruffy, and Felix put up with every one albeit reluctantly at first. Tragedy struck when Felix became stricken with cancer of the kidneys. Under constant care of the vet his sufferings were held back as long as possible. However, one afternoon the vet attempted to convince Tracy that the poor cat felt so nauseous and ill that his life had no quality. The kind doctor advised the family to put Felix to sleep. He'd had an active and full life, though certainly not as long as any of them would have wished. The family held a council meeting, and decided to end Felix's misery. The three of them went together to the vet's with Tracy's holding Felix, and when the nurse reached for Felix, Felix turned his huge grape green eyes upon Tracy's face for the last time with a look of such trust and love as though saying I know you're taking care of me. This seemed to be the only way Tracy could stand to think about it.

After Felix's death the family adopted three more cats in turn. First when Eric was attending college, he rescued a tabby the family named Lollipop from a traffic-filled street in South Orange. Barely old enough to leave its mother. Lollipop crossed a street humming with angry, honking cars, and Eric ran out into the middle of the street and swept Lollipop up into his arms. Lolly led a happy life, although he became the oil to Georgette's water. Sadly, one day both cats contracted leukemia, and Georgette ran away to die as was her wont whenever she was sick, and the family nursed Lolly even giving him transfusions to prolong his life at the vet's suggestion. He lived quite a while thanks to the pampering and care he received. Because of the leukemia, the family had to wait six months before they could adopt another cat to be sure the germ had disappeared from the environment. However when finally the house had been disinfected Kevin saw a notice on the bulletin board from the A& P about two homeless kittens from the same litter. Their coloring according to the notice was black and black multi. Figuring this meant black and white it seemed a good omen, and Kevin with the family's blessing went and carted home a box containing two black cats, later named Nefer and Miew—Egyptian names meaning beautiful and cat. Although Miew appeared sleek and the more beautiful of the two, Nefer exhibited courage and ingenuity to make up for her lack of beauty or size. For a while when Miew usurped all the attention, she collected Tracy's slips, a candle holder, and a knickknack of Kevin's and kept them under the bed for comfort. When Tracy misplaced an article of clothing she merely looked under the bed.

Miew proved to be lazy and conceited barely moving from the couch except for meals. Tracy often said that had Miew been their first cat he would have been their last cat. However, Felix the Cat had been the premiere cat, and his star qualities would cause this family to always harbor a furry friend under their roof.

THE DRAMA CLUB

PRESENTS

"KIND LADY"

Samantha sauntered toward the auditorium walking in small steps because she prayed as she moved. She hoped to get a super part in the play, "KIND LADY", for which the Drama Club had called try-outs starting in moments. Her eyes didn't rest solely upon the lead role, although she'd play that with aplomb if asked. Mila, the Drama Club's star actress, always landed the major plum role. Samantha acknowledged that Mila could act although she found her to be almost flamboyant at times. This play had a large cast chock full of character parts. Many of the parts could be outstanding especially if handled right. The choicest character role advertised for someone to play the kind lady's closest friend and partner in countless bridge games and shared cups of tea. The character possessed strong moral traits and even stronger opinions, and could be played to the hilt. Capping off the opportunities to show this friend's forceful personality, the role called for this persona to be first on the stage alone for a few minutes. What a bonanza for an actress.

Samantha made her decision. She'd throw all her energies towards winning the part of the close friend and confidant. She took the time to notice that this character's name came directly below that of the lead-the kind lady. Second notice and an appearance first alone on the stage would be hard to beat. Now she felt psyched. During Mila's try-out, Samantha studied the script looking for a way to showcase her part. Not too many people tried out for the kind lady part, so too soon she found herself on the stage actually trying out for the imperious friend. She read with empathy for the role and discovered to her delight that most of her fellow Drama Club members appeared to be listening to the reading with rapt expressions. Before leaving the auditorium that same afternoon, Samantha learned that she'd bagged the role she'd tried out for. She felt set to roll. Today's being Friday, the first rehearsal and the beginning of this show business venture would start Monday afternoon after classes.

When Samantha woke on Monday morning, her throat scratched when she swallowed, and her skin felt burning to the touch. Her voice came forth as a croak. When her mother looked at her at the breakfast table she ordered,

"Samantha, for goodness sake, go back to bed. You have a fever. The flu is raging all around the school, and you refused to have a shot. I forbid you to go to school."

"Mother, this is the first day of rehearsal. If I don't show I'll miss the rhythm established at the start. Everyone will be ahead of me in proficiency. I might even get replaced."

"Save the dramatics for the play, Greta Garbo. You'll need them when you do go back to school and attend the rehearsals."

For five agonizing days, a whole school week, Samantha tossed and rebelled in bed. She kept up with her homework, but the closest she could get to the play was a daily telephone call from Liz who also had a part. Since she had time, Samantha used it to memorize the part. She might arrive late for rehearsals, but she'd know her part and not need the script. Walking to school with Liz on the following Monday morning, a whole week later than she'd planned to go to rehearsals, Samantha quizzed her about each aspect concerning the play.

"Mila is emoting beautifully. The rest of us are trying to decide whether to use English or Cockney accents for our roles. Mr. Deeds said not to unless we could do them with a fair semblance of accuracy. The audience will laugh if the accents are off. Mr. Deeds said better to do it plain in our own accents than to screw up the English accents."

"He's right, Liz. I'm going to do it straight. I bet you use the English accent since your ear is so good. You sing like an angel. I bet you have an ear for language too."

"Yes," Liz acquiesced, "I'm doing a Cockney accent."

The hands on the large round school classroom clocks moved laboriously all day. Finally at the stroke of three Samantha galloped into the auditorium and discovered herself to be the first to arrive at rehearsal. She bumped into Mr. Deeds who entered the auditorium almost immediately and he said,

"So glad to have you here at last. You look so bright and anxious to begin. Good. Let's see what you can do. We could start your scene alone on stage even before the rest of the cast arrives."

Samantha bounded onto the stage before the words were out of his mouth. She plunged into her opening speech. Mr. Deeds seemed excited to note that she spoke without her script. Apparently, this constituted a first for the Drama Club in this play. Before she'd finished her speech, Mila, Liz and the rest of the super-sized cast arrived, and Samantha's real life started. No routine she'd ever experienced pleased and exhilarated Samantha as much as being involved with rehearsals for an upcoming play did. Although the Drama Club members had put on many productions since Samantha found herself with the coveted Drama Club invitation sitting on her desk the Monday after Drama Club try-outs, never before had they produced a play to be shown at night for money to be collected at the door with the proceeds to go to the Drama Club. This event qualified as a big deal. Most rewarding of all, Samantha felt to be the close comradery among the cast. By opening night she knew they'd feel towards each other like brothers and sisters bound together by their wanting the play to succeed which seemed as close as blood ties. Although this closeness usually only lasted for the run of the play, it remained real just the same. They labored together during rehearsals trying to buoy each other up as Mr. Deeds distributed advice to better their performances.

Samantha's character had a climatic scene at the end of the second act, after which her character's unfortunate demise in a plane crash gets discussed by the rest of the cast. This scene called for Samantha to roll off her tongue the words "get rid of the wretches!" in a commanding tone as she exits the stage. The words contain extreme importance since this domineering friend of the kind lady seems to be the only character who realizes what real danger the kind lady has fallen into. Mr. Deeds worked with Samantha to get a really authoritarian tone into her voice so as to project extreme confidence in this character's abilities to the sympathetic audience. The rest of the cast cheered her on as she labored on perfecting the scene, which Mr. Deeds seemed to feel pivotal to the entire outcome of the play.

Samantha had a few run-ins with Mila during the course of rehearsals, one scene where the two characters appear together, the girls planned to wear gowns. Prior to dress rehearsal, fortunately, the girls modeled their choices, and Mila threw a temper tantrum because she felt that the red brocade Samantha wore clashed with her pink gown. This, she seemed to feel, would not do. However, Mr. Deeds intervened asking Samantha whether or not she owned a black lace shawl. Samantha did indeed own such a thing by virtue of her grandmother's benevolence, and she promised to bring it to the next rehearsal. The lace shawl muted the brocade gown, and any clashing colors no longer seemed visible to the rest of the cast. Hair styles posed the next problem with Mila's demanding first choice to wear her hair up and deciding that Samantha's hair should fall normally to her shoulders. Again, Mr. Deeds broke in saying that Samantha should feel free to wear her hair however she decided she wanted it. Samantha's ire burned hot inside her, but Mr. Deeds's championship helped her to keep it inside. She felt it to be bad enough for Mila to always snatch the choicest parts without her lording her prominence over the rest of the cast. Samantha's thoughts kept sneaking to an inner feeling of hers that Mila picked on her more than anyone else. She reconciled herself to this thought by realizing that it would mean if true that Mila feared her work more than the efforts of the other members of the cast. This represented quite a coup. Samantha decided to ignore Mila's petty behavior and expend her energies throwing herself into her character.

Dress rehearsal arrived, and true to legend the cast performed dismally. Mr. Deeds even picked on Samantha's performance reminding her again of how regal she must sound as she exited the stage throwing her last remark over her shoulder.

"You may toss the line off as you exit, but the impact of what you say should reverberate through the minds of the audience. You want them to mark this advice."

"I'll try Mr. Deeds, but I don't think I can perform any better."

"Nonsense!"

Nerves frayed and raw with terror causing her to block out her whole first scene, Samantha waited back stage for curtain call. Her being first and alone on the stage when the curtain opened made her mouth dry and her body tremble so that she almost fell of the wing chair where she sat on the stage supposedly with her dignity intact.

She nearly fainted when the stage manager said one moment as she'd forgotten every line including her first words. An instant later the curtain opened, and she blossomed coming alive in the full ripeness of her performance. The advice that Mr. Deeds had poured over her like a cooling shower of water came to her aid now making her creativity bloom. All through the first act and into the second she grew with confidence prodding her performance, and when the time came for her turning point of the play line, she delivered it with savior faire causing Mr. Deeds to smile and say, "Bravo," as she exited. "I'm proud of you, Samantha."

Unfortunately, during the third act the perfection of the play began to topple. Samantha had ambiguous feelings about this, since her part in the play had ended on such a high note. However, her sympathy for the rest of the cast as well as her real concern for the good of the play made her cheer them on. The blot on the perfection of the play was a piece of scenery's smashing as one of the characters exited through a scenery door. The door came crashing down, and the audience poured forth nervous laughter. The cast pulled themselves together, and indeed performed better than the roles called for to compensate for the faulty scenery's intrusion into their production. The cast party after the play brought fun for the entire cast, and Samantha even flirted with a fellow cast member, Dennis, who had had a crush on her for the run of the play. She felt it would be safe to flirt with him now as with the curtain falling on the play, the curtain would also fall on their togetherness soon. They had to wait a week for the notices as the school newspaper didn't publish every day, but the notices proved worth waiting for. "Kind Lady" had been kind to Samantha with the newspaper singling out her performance for special commendation denoting more space raving about her performance than they gave to

Mila. What a wow. She felt glad to have decided upon reaching for the goal of the friend. The role had been friendly to her as well as kind.

ABOUT THE AUTHOR

Barto, Susan C. **Born:** 6/21/41 **Parents:** Eda and William Forcellon. **Spouse:** Harry W. Barto. **Children:** William M. Barto. **Education:** Katherine Gibbs School—Union College, NJ. **Occupation:** Legal Secretary—Legislative Aide; Last 10 yrs I have been a writer. **Memberships:** Raritan Valley College Book Group—Currently President Friends of the Hunterdon Museum of Art—New Providence Library Board—NJ. **Honors:** Golden Certificate Award, Drury's Publishing—Plaque when I left Library Board. Listed in 1999/2000 Who's Who In the east, and 2000 Who's Who in America. **Personal Note:** Married to husband, Harry. One son, William. I love to write. Writing defines who I am. **Publishing Credits:** Twelve stories published with Creative With Words, One story published with Yesterday's Magazette—one story published with Writer's Guidelines & News, One story published Good Old Days, one story Reminisce, one story Book The Fabulous Fifties. Four printed books and one eBook of stories published by Drury's Publishing™,

Many stories published with Drury's Publishing—Extensive travel, Egypt, Italy, England and France.